Gaston Leroux's
Phantom Stories

GASTON LEROUX

Le
Fantôme
de l'Opéra

Gaston Leroux's Phantom Stories

Grand Guignol Tales
by the author of
The Phantom of the Opera

COMPILED & INTRODUCED
BY PETER HAINING

the apocryphile press
BERKELEY, CA
www.apocryphile.org

apocryphile press
BERKELEY, CA

Apocryphile Press
1700 Shattuck Ave #81
Berkeley, CA 94709
www.apocryphile.org

First published in London, England
by Victor Gollancz, Ltd.
Copyright 1980 by Peter Haining.
First Apocryphile edition, 2006.

ISBN 1-933993-05-7

Printed in the United States of America

CONTENTS

ACKNOWLEDGEMENTS

The stories in this collection originally appeared in French and English publications as follows: "A Terrible Tale" as *Un Histoire Epouvantable* in *Le Coeur Cambriole*, November 1922; "The Mystery of the Four Husbands" in *Weird Tales*, December, 1929; "The Inn of Terror" in *Weird Tales*, August, 1929; "The Woman with the Velvet Collar" in *Weird Tales*, October, 1929; "The Crime on Christmas Night" in *Weird Tales*, December 1930; "In Letters of Fire" in *Je Sais Tout*, March 1908; "The Gold Axe" in *Touche a Tout*, February, 1912; "The Waxwork Museum" in *Le Coeur Cambriole*, November 1922; and "The Real Opera Ghost" 'in *Le Fantome de l'Opera* 1911. Not all the translators were credited, but acknowledgement is due to Hannaford Bennett, Mildred Prochet, Morris Bentinck, and Alexander Peters. The editor also extends his thanks to the following for their help in locating the stories as well as providing information about the elusive author and his work: Frank Parnell, Bill Lofts, Ken Chapman, Bill Blackbeard, and Colin G, Davis.

The Master of Grand Guignol

GASTON LEROUX'S *The Phantom of the Opera* (1911) is not only considered one of the half-dozen great classic novels of horror, but was also the inspiration of a film made in 1925 which has influenced almost every subsequent picture in the terror genre. Yet for all its fame – the title is surely as familiar as *Frankenstein* or *Dracula* – the book is today largely unread, that remarkable early movie only rarely shown, and the author himself almost completely forgotten. There are many people who visit the enormous, fantastic and beautiful edifice of the Paris Opera House in the Place de l'Opéra, the setting of the story, unaware of the connection, or of the fact that the novel is based on a mysterious figure who once actually lived in the cavernous underworld of chambers and passageways where – so legend has it – a small lake lies hidden deep beneath the luxurious auditorium and stage.

Though the original novel is little read, the basic plot is widely familiar, no doubt due to the series of film versions of the story. Somewhere in the labyrinth of the Opéra lives the Phantom, seemingly possessed with the power to move stage scenery at will, to strike performers dumb, and appear and disappear whenever he chooses. He falls in love with a beautiful, demure young singer named Christine Daaé, whom he determines to make into a great opera star. Unable to reveal himself to her, he uses his mysterious voice to convince her he is the "Angel of Music", and then proceeds to fulfil his objective. But at the moment of his triumph, the girl falls in love with the dashing Vicomte de Chagny, and in a fit of jealousy the Phantom carries her off to his secret hiding-place on the underground lake. There, frightened but curious about her strange masked captor, the girl suddenly pulls off his mask to expose the hideously deformed face beneath. It is a scene which has become a classic moment both in literature and on the screen. Only then do we learn of the Phantom's history and his unhappy life, the details of which are related by an equally mysterious man known only as "The Persian". These I shall withhold here in the hope that the reader might care to turn to the original and find out for himself!

When Universal Pictures decided to film *The Phantom of the Opera* in 1925, they chose for the leading role of Erik, the Phantom, Lon Chaney, a former vaudeville comedian and bit part actor. (This was prior to their making the Bela Lugosi and Boris Karloff versions of *Dracula* and *Frankenstein* in the Thirties, which made them famous as horror movie makers and initiated a world-wide cult.) Chaney was particularly skilled as a make-up artist, and he had already achieved a major success as the terribly crippled Quasimodo in *The Hunchback of Notre Dame* (1923), which involved his wearing an excruciatingly painful costume. When work began on shooting the Leroux novel, a story leaked out that the make-up Chaney had devised for himself was so horrible that the picture would probably never be publicly shown. It provided good publicity, and the film was an enormous financial success, as well as earning critical acclaim and having far-reaching effects on all later horror films, including the whole string of classics made by Universal themselves in the Thirties. The picture was also something of a landmark in its introduction of Technicolor for certain scenes, including the Masked Ball where the Phantom appears dressed as the Red Death.

Writing of Lon Chaney's performance in his *History of the Horror Film* (1967), Carlos Clarens has said, "Whether reported faintings in the audience were real or dreamed up by the Universal publicity department, Chaney's characterisation was everything the public had come to expect of him. In a daily, self-imposed ordeal, Chaney's features were distended, pulled apart, and disfigured into a livid, cadaverous face of Death itself." (Vividly illustrated in a still from the film that appears on the dust jacket of this book.) Later, as a result of further similar roles, Chaney was to become known as "The Man of a Thousand Faces".

While *The Phantom of the Opera* established Lon Chaney as a world star, it initially did little for the man who had created the original story. Gaston Leroux was ill at his Paris home at the time the picture was being made in Hollywood, and played no part in its creation. Indeed, he had only two years left to live, and it is doubtful whether he ever saw the film. None the less, with the passage of time, it was to play an important part in carving a niche for him in both screen and literary history.

The Phantom was not the first of Leroux's stories to have been filmed. The first was a silent version of his detective thriller, *The Mystery of the Yellow Room*, made in France within a year of the book's publication in 1907. This story is a milestone in the detective story genre, being one of the very first "locked room" mysteries, in which a seemingly impossible crime occurs in a hermetically sealed room. The central figure in the story is a precocious teenage reporter-cum-amateur-detective named Joseph Rouletabille who, after the case has baffled the best minds in the Paris police force, solves the mystery of how a girl was assaulted and wounded in the room. Leroux was himself a journalist, and also had an intimate knowledge of the workings of the law; this enabled him to write an authentic and exciting thriller still eminently readable today. Another important feature of the book is Leroux's use of what was later to become a popular device in detective fiction – the final exposure of the criminal as the least likely person among all the suspects. *The Mystery of the Yellow Room* was filmed several times during the silent era, the best version being that made in America by Realart in 1919, with Lorin Baker as Rouletabille. Although Leroux wrote several other novels featuring Rouletabille, only the sequel to the first book, which was called *The Perfume of the Lady in Black* (1911), was turned into a movie. It was filmed in 1912 by the French director, Maurice Tourneur.

In 1913, the French film company Eclair took up another of Leroux's stories which had just been serialised in a newspaper. This was *Balaoo*, about a scientist called Dr Coriolis who transforms an enormous baboon into a half-humanised monster. Predictably, the monster escapes, attempts to abduct a beautiful girl to become his mate, and is finally caught in a trap and killed. A feature of the film was the skilful portrayal of Balaoo by an actor called Lucien Bataille. In Britain and America the film was retitled *The Demon Baboon*, and billed as "the fantastic tale of the Weirdest Animal Ever Created!" In 1927, the American film company Twentieth Century Fox was attracted to Leroux's story, and remade it as *The Wizard* with Gustav von Seyffertitz as Dr Coriolis and George Kotsonaros as the baboon man. Unfortunately no copy of this film is known to have survived, and it has been described by the movie historian William K. Everson as "the most fascinating, elusive and sought-after of all 'lost' films". Fox might almost be suspected of having foreseen what was going to happen to this picture, for in 1942 they filmed the story yet again, retitled *Dr Renault's Secret*. This version still exists and contains a sinister performance by George Zucco as the scientist, and J. Carroll Naish as a most moving Balaoo.

Another of Leroux's later literary creations, Chéri-Bibi, a mysterious magician who initially turns criminal to prove himself innocent of the charge of murdering his father and then becomes a crime fighter, has also been brought to the screen twice. The first version, made by M.G.M. in 1931, was entitled *The Phantom of Paris* (no doubt to take advantage of the success of Universal's earlier picture), and starred John Gilbert as the magician and Leila Hyams as his girlfriend Cecily, who features in all his literary adventures. The story was re-filmed in France in 1937, with Pierre Fresnay as Chéri-Bibi.

After its initial appearance in 1925, *The Phantom of the Opera* was again filmed by Universal in 1943, using lush Technicolor throughout and starring Claude Rains – it got an Academy Award; then by Hammer Films in Britain with Herbert Lom (1962); and most recently in America by Twentieth Century Fox, who converted the setting of the story from the Paris Opera House to a contemporary rock and roll theatre in New York! William Finlay starred in this remake which was retitled *Phantom of the Paradise* (1974).

Having looked briefly at the most visible signs of Gaston Leroux's literary creations, what sort of man was the author himself? His is yet another case of a writer eclipsed by his creation, just as Sir Arthur Conan Doyle must forever live in the shadow of Sherlock Holmes. Probably few among the millions of people in whose minds the frightening masked figure of Erik is deeply etched, could correctly name his literary begetter. Fewer still know anything of the author's life. Like the Phantom's eventual fate in the dank, gloomy underworld of the Opera House, his memory has been consigned to oblivion. Yet Leroux, lawyer, journalist, traveller, a man who faced death on numerous occasions, was in many ways as interesting as the thrilling, ingenious and always entertaining stories he wrote.

Gaston Leroux was born in Paris in August 1868, the only son of modestly well-to-do parents who owned a clothing shop not far from the Champs Elysées. As a child he was high-spirited and wilful, invariably the leader in any group of youngsters and always the first to initiate any daring prank. He apparently had several skirmishes with the local gendarmerie, but got into trouble for misdemeanours rather than actual crimes. A story that he once thought about running away from home to join a gang of criminals operating from a hide-out in Montmartre seems most likely to have been invented by him later in life to give a little extra colour to his autobiography.

His school career was undistinguished, although he showed a natural ability for composition and was fond of geography. After he left school his father managed to secure him a position in a firm of lawyers who were related to the Leroux's. Young Gaston was evidently far from happy at this occupation, which mainly involved his copying long drafts and depositions in copperplate handwriting, but it did give him an insight into the legal world which was to prove useful later on. In his spare time, when he was not out with friends in the boulevard cafés, he occupied himself writing essays and stories. A few of these he submitted to small magazines and weekly newspapers, and was overjoyed when they were published. The fact that he did not get paid for most of them mattered little at this time!

In 1890 he managed to get a new job as a legal chronicler on one of the Paris newspapers. He told his employers he had qualified as a lawyer, and whether this was true or not he was soon demonstrating a considerable skill in reporting legal matters and covering interesting or sensational court cases. He had also become fascinated with the theatre and begged his editor to let him cover the opening nights of some of the new plays in the capital. This interest made him try his hand at being a dramatist, and although he subsequently wrote a number of plays, only those written in collaboration with more experienced playwrights enjoyed real success. Among these can be counted *Alsace*, written with Camille Dreyfus and performed at the Théâtre Réjane, and *Le Lys* with Pierre Wolff, which was put on at the Théâtre du Vaudeville. *La Maison des Juges*, a three-act drama which Leroux wrote on his own, was staged at l'Odéon and earned some critical acclaim as well as running for almost six months. Leroux also claimed in his biographical notes to have been a "writer on hygiene", though I have been unable to find any items attributable to him to explain what he meant by this intriguing reference.

It was when he became a full-time correspondent that Leroux's life entered its most exciting phase. With *carte blanche* to travel where he pleased in search of stories, he sought out international dramas – political upheavals, border incidents and wars – throughout Europe, and further afield. At last he was able to slake the restlessness he had felt since childhood, journeying on land and sea, and hardly a week passed by without his despatching some exciting story back to Paris.

In the years up to the turn of the century – to quote Stanley J. Kunitz and Howard Haycraft in *Twentieth Century Authors* (1950) – "Leroux tramped up and down the world, his daring spirit carrying him into faraway corners and into and out of a dozen scrapes". His travels took him from Finland to Nijni Novgorod and south to the Caspian Sea, and through Italy, Egypt and Morocco. Because of the hostility usually displayed towards Europeans in certain of these places, Leroux made a habit of disguising himself in order to be able to witness events at first hand. According to his own account, while he was in Morocco he disguised himself as an Arab, and on several occasions at Larache and in Fez he ran the very real danger of losing his life. This knowledge of disguise was to help him later in the writing of his mysteries, including *The Phantom of the Opera* and *Man of a Hundred Faces*.

The stories he obtained made him popular with newspaper editors and readers, and the renowned French journal, *L'Illustration*, dubbed him "the eternal reporter". It was said he could get a story out of the most unlikely situations and from the most difficult people. A frequently quoted tale about him among French journalists concerned his attempt to interview the Colonial Secretary, Joseph Chamberlain, during the South African War. By a combination of stealth and boldness Leroux managed to get into Chamberlain's private study, and sat down in a seat opposite the statesman's desk to await his arrival. Unfortunately just before Chamberlain arrived a secretary came into the room and, seeing the unwelcome intruder, quickly ordered him out of the building. Leroux was not altogether dismayed and quickly turned out a three-column article, "How I Failed To See Chamberlain", which was hailed as "a little masterpiece of good humour and wit"!

It is perhaps not surprising, after such adventures, that Leroux should think of using his experiences as the basis for some novels, and in the early 1900s he started to write a series of unashamedly sensational yarns, all heavily laced with mystery and terror. Early works like *La Double Vie de Théophraste Longuet*, a kind of French *Dr Jekyll and Mr Hyde*, and *La Bataille Invisible*, about a madman's scheme to rule the world, revealed him as a storyteller of ingenuity and excitement.

In 1907 he scored his first major success with the publication of *Le Mystère de la Chambre Jaune*, which introduced to the public the brilliant young detective Rouletabille and his admiring chronicler, Sainclair, who is reminiscent of Dr Watson. Howard Haycraft, the expert on crime fiction has underlined the achievement of this book in his *Murder For Pleasure: The Life and Times of the Detective Story* (1942):

The Mystery of the Yellow Room is generally recognised, on
the strength of its central puzzle, as one of the classic examples
of the genre. For sheer plot manipulation and ratiocination –
no simpler word will describe the quality of its Gallic logic – it
has seldom been surpassed. It remains, after a generation of
imitation, the most brilliant of all "locked room" novels. The
author's use of the official detective as the culprit (though an
outworn device today) was also in its time a highly original
conception.

Despite this praise, Mr Haycraft goes on to say the book has
numerous faults, including poor characterisation and undue re-
liance on coincidence, and he believes that Leroux's importance
today is "chiefly historical and technical". None of the other
books he wrote about Rouletabille enjoyed anything like the
success of *The Mystery of the Yellow Room*, which was swiftly
translated into English and published with resounding success on
both sides of the Atlantic.*

The second and most important milestone in Leroux's literary
career came in 1911, when he published *La Fantôme de l'Opéra*,
although this did not receive the immediate acclaim which the
Rouletabille novel had done. It did, however, sell well in volume
form, and was serialised in French, English and American newspapers. Leroux had got the idea for the novel during one of his
many visits as a critic to the Paris Opera House. He heard the
legend of a mysterious man who was supposed to live in the
subterranean depths of the building and had been responsible for
some strange deaths. His reporter's instinct told him that here
was a very special story and he busied himself researching all the
facts he could find. I have reprinted at the end of this volume
Leroux's own account of how he came to write the novel, *The
Real Opera Ghost.*

* The complete list of titles which make up the series of Leroux's
Aventures Extraordinaires de Joseph Rouletabille, reporteur is: *Le·
Mystère de la Chambre Jaune*; *Le Parfum de la Dame en Noir*;
Rouletabille chez le Tsar; *Le Château Noir (Rouletabille à la Guerre)*;
Les Étranges Noces de Rouletabille; *Rouletabille chez Krupp*; *Le Crime
de Rouletabille* and *Rouletabille chez les Bohémiens.*

The enormous edifice of the Opera House which had been conceived during the glorious days of the Empire, in 1861, but not completed until 1879, was a marvellous background for Leroux's story. He made the most of its seventeen floors, vast maze of stairways and corridors, innumerable dressing rooms to cater for over five hundred performers, and the dozens of storage cellars for scenery and costumes. The fact that the lower levels of the place were vast and empty, rarely visited or explored, made the tale that he spun around the mysterious phantom all the more intriguing and exciting. It was clearly a unique creation, and the only surprise is that its importance was some time in being appreciated, and that its reputation was made on the screen rather than in print.

With *The Phantom of the Opera* Leroux reached the height of his literary powers, and although he developed another fascinating figure, Chéri-Bibi, the magician, who appeared in several novels between 1916 and 1923,* nothing quite matched that one book. He did produce several more grim and exciting novels in the same vein, such as *Balaoo*, *The Man with the Black Feather* (1912) and *The Man Who Came Back from the Dead* (1916) both about reincarnation; *The Secret of the Night* (1914) and *Bride of the Sun* (1915) two imaginative fantasies; and the posthumously published works, *Man of a Hundred Faces* (1930) and *The Haunted Chair* (1931). He also wrote a small number of really outstanding macabre and weird short stories which are even less well-known and more neglected than his novels – and it is a selection of the best of these which I have collected together in this anthology.

Most of these stories were written in the early 1920s when Leroux's popularity was at its peak, and the demands for his work were never-ending. As a thoroughly professional journalist and a man never afraid of hard work, he did not like refusing requests, and drew on his seemingly bottomless well of ideas for the stories. All are the equal of, if not actually superior to, most of his longer novels.

* The important Chéri-Bibi novels are: *Les Cages Flottantes*; *Chéri-Bibi et Cecily*; *Palas et Chéri-Bibi* and *Fatalitas!*

A group of these tales takes the form of adventures related by five old sea captains who meet in a café at Toulon to try and outdo each other with yarns from their past. I have selected one tale by each of them for this book. The remaining stories demonstrate Leroux's mastery of three other areas of fiction which particularly fascinated him: historical subjects ("In Letters of Fire"), the mixture of romance and terror ("The Gold Axe") and a macabre drama woven around the Paris he knew and loved ("The Waxwork Museum").

The adventurous and hectic life that the big, heavily-bearded Leroux had enjoyed eventually took its toll on his health, and by 1925, when he was fifty-seven, he had become a sick man. His eyesight, which had never been particularly good (although he tried to deny the fact, and said he only wore gold-rimmed pince-nez to be fashionable), also started to fail. Despite the success of his books and the films made from them, he was never a wealthy man; the fact that he was described as one of the most popular French mystery writers of the time seemed to give him more personal satisfaction than any financial reward might have done. Nothing could deter him from working, however, and he did not completely lay down his pen until the day of his death on 16 April 1927.

Fashions in both the detective and the horror novel seem quickly to leave behind both his Rouletabille stories and *The Phantom of the Opera*, and it was some years before *The Mystery of the Yellow Room* was recognised as a classic *tour de force*, and the story of the masked man appreciated as one of the greatest contributions to the genre of macabre fiction. In my contention Gaston Leroux was more than just a brilliant writer of weird fiction, he was a master of Grand Guignol. It is my hope that the republication of the stories in this collection, stories which have been unobtainable for over half a century, will encourage a rediscovery and reassessment of all his work beyond that one grim figure that still haunts us all – Erik, The Phantom of the Opera.

PETER HAINING
September 1979

A TERRIBLE TALE

CAPTAIN MICHEL HAD but one arm, which he found useful when he lit his pipe. He was an old sea-dog whose acquaintance, with that of four other old salts, I made one evening on the open front of a café in the Vieille Darse, Toulon, where I was taking an appetiser. And in this way we fell into the habit of foregathering over a glass within a stone's throw of the rippling waves and the swinging dinghys, about the hour when the sun sinks behind Tamaris.

The four old mariners were known as Zinzin, Dorat – Captain Dorat – Bagatelle, and Chaulieu – that old fellow Chaulieu. They had, of course, sailed every sea and met with a thousand adventures; and now that they were retired on their pensions, they spent their time telling each other terrible tales.

Captain Michel alone never indulged in any reminiscences. And as he seemed in no way surprised by anything he heard, his old comrades in the end grew exasperated with him.

"Look here, Captain Michel, hasn't anything out of the way ever happened to you?"

"Oh yes," the captain made answer, taking his pipe from his mouth. "Yes, something happened to me once – just once."

"Well, let's have it."

"No."

"Why not?"

"Because it's too awful. You might not be able to stand it. I've often tried to tell the story but people have slipped away before I finished it."

The four sea-dogs vied with each other in the loudness of their guffaws, declaring that Captain Michel was trying to find some excuse, because in reality, nothing extraordinary had ever happened to him.

The old fellow stared at them a moment, and then suddenly

accepting the situation, laid his pipe on the table. This unusual gesture was in itself startling!

"Messieurs, I'll tell you how I lost my arm," he began.

"In those days – some twenty years ago – I owned a small villa, in the suburb of Le Mourillon, which had been left to me, for my family were long settled in these parts and I myself was born here.

"It suited me to take a little rest after a long voyage and before setting sail again. For that matter, I rather liked the place, and lived quite peaceably among seafaring men and colonials who troubled me very little, and whom I rarely saw, occupied as they were as a rule in opium-smoking with their lady friends, or with other business which did not concern me. Of course there is no accounting for tastes, but as long as they didn't interfere with me, I was satisfied . . .

"It so happened that one night they did interfere with my habit of going to sleep. I was awakened with a start by an extraordinary uproar, the meaning of which I couldn't possibly make out. I had left my window open as usual. I listened in a state of bewilderment to a tremendous din, which was a cross between the rumbling of thunder and the roll of a drum, but such a drum! It was as though a couple of hundred drumsticks were being madly beaten, not on ordinary drumskin, but on a wooden drum.

"The disturbance came from the villa opposite, which had been empty for some five years, and on which I had noticed, the previous evening, a board bearing the announcement: 'To be sold'.

"I let my gaze stray from the window of my bedroom, on the first floor, beyond the small garden in which the house stood, and my eye took in every door and window, even the doors and windows on the ground floor. They were still closed as I had seen them during the day; but I caught sight of gleams of light through the chinks in the shutters on the ground floor. Who and what were these people? How had they found their way into this solitary house at the far end of Le Mourillon? What sort of company was it that had obtained admission into this deserted dwelling, and why were they kicking up such a shindy?

"The extraordinary din, like the thunderous beating of a wooden drum, continued. It went on for another hour, and then as dawn was breaking, the front door opened, and there appeared in the doorway the most radiant creature that I have ever beheld. She was clad in a low-necked dress, and held with perfect grace a lamp whose beams fell over the shoulders of a goddess. I distinctly heard her say in the echoing night, while a kind and gentle smile flickered across her face:

" 'Goodbye, dear friend, till next year.'

"To whom was she speaking? It was impossible for me to tell for I could see no one standing beside her. She remained at the entrance holding the lamp for some minutes, until the garden gate opened by itself and closed by itself. Then the front door of the house was shut in its turn, and I saw nothing more.

"It seemed to me that I was either losing my head or was the sport of a dream, for I knew that it was out of the question for anyone to pass through the garden without my perceiving him.

"I was still planted at the window, incapable of the least movement or thought, when the door of the house opened a second time, and the same vision of beauty appeared still carrying a lamp and still alone.

" 'Hush,' she said. 'Don't make a noise any of you. We mustn't disturb our neighbour opposite. I'll come with you.'

"And silently and alone she crossed the garden and stopped at the gate on which the full rays of the lamp shone; so much so, indeed, that I clearly saw the knob of the gate turn of its own accord without any hand being placed upon it. And the gate opened once again by itself in the presence of this woman who, moreover, did not evince any surprise. Need I explain that from where I was posted, I could see both in front and behind the gate; in other words, that I saw it sideways?

"This 'splendid apparition' made a charming movement of her head towards the empty darkness which the glare of the lamp made visible; then she smiled and said:

" 'Well, goodbye until next year. My husband is very pleased. Not a single one of you failed to answer the call. Goodbye, messieurs.'

"And I heard several voices in unison:

" 'Goodbye, madame, goodbye, dear madame, until next year.'

"And as the mysterious hostess was preparing to close the door herself, I heard a voice:

" 'Oh, please, don't trouble.'

"And the door was once more closed.

"The next moment the air was filled with a curious sound; it was like the chirping of a flock of birds, and it seemed as if this beautiful woman had opened the cage of a whole brood of house sparrows.

"She quietly walked back to the house. The lights on the ground floor were then out, but I noticed a glimmer in the windows of the first floor.

"When she reached the house she said:

" 'Are you upstairs, Gérard?'

"I could not hear the answer, but the front door was again closed, and a few minutes later the light on the first floor went out.

"I was still standing at my window at eight o'clock in the morning, staring in blank amazement at the house and garden which had revealed such strange happenings in darkness, and which now in the full light of day assumed their familiar aspect. The garden was a waste, and the house itself seemed as desolate as it was the day before.

"So much so, indeed, that when I told my old charwoman, who had just come, of the queer events which I had witnessed, she tapped my forehead with her dirty forefinger and muttered that I had smoked one pipe too many. Now I have never been a smoker of opium, and her answer gave me a good opportunity of sacking the old sloven whom I had for some time wanted to get rid of, and who came for a couple of hours each day to 'clean up' the place for me. For that matter I did not need anyone, as I was setting sail again next day.

"I barely had time to put my things together, make a few purchases, say farewell to my friends, and catch the train for Le Havre. I had fixed up an appointment with the Transatlantic company which would keep me away from Toulon for some eleven or twelve months.

"In due course I returned to Toulon, but though I had refrained from mentioning my adventure to a soul, I still continued to think of it. The vision of the lady of the lamp obsessed me wherever I went, and the last words which she uttered to her unseen friends still rang in my ears:

" 'Well, goodbye until next year.'

"And I never ceased to think of the meeting. I, too, was determined to be there and to discover, at whatever cost, the solution of a mystery which was intensely perplexing to a sensible man like myself, who did not believe in ghosts or phantom beings.

"Unfortunately I was soon to learn that neither heaven nor hell were concerned in the terrible story.

"It was six o'clock in the evening when I set foot again in my house at Toulon; and it was two days before the anniversary of the wonderful night.

"The first thing that I did on going inside was to run up to my room and open the window. It was summer and broad daylight, and my eyes at once fell upon a lady of great beauty who was placidly walking about gathering flowers in the garden of the house opposite. At the noise made by the opening window she looked up.

"It was the lady of the lamp. I recognised her, and she seemed not less beautiful by day than by night. Her skin was as white as the teeth of an African negro, her eyes bluer than the waters at Tamaris, her hair as soft and fair as the finest flax.

"Why should I not make the confession? When I beheld this woman of whom I had been dreaming for a year, a strange feeling came over me. She was no illusion of a diseased imagination. She stood before me in the flesh; and every window of the house was open and flower-bedecked by her hands. There was nothing fantastic in all this.

"She caught sight of me and at once displayed some degree of annoyance. She walked a few steps farther in the centre path of the garden, and then shrugging her shoulders as though she were disconcerted said:

"'Let's go in, Gérard. I'm beginning to feel the coolness of the night.'

"I let my gaze stray round the garden. I could perceive no one. To whom was she speaking? . . . Nobody there!

"Then was she mad? It scarcely seemed so.

"I watched her return to the house. She passed into it, the door was closed, and she at once shut the windows.

"I did not see or hear anything worth noticing that night. Next morning at ten o'clock I observed my neighbour leaving the garden attired as if for a walk. She locked the gate after her and set out in the direction of Toulon.

"I started off in my turn. Pointing to the fashionably dressed figure in front of me I asked the first tradesman whom I met if he knew the lady's name.

"'Why, of course. She's your neighbour. She is living with her husband at the Villa Makoko. They moved in about a year ago, just as you went away. They are regular boors. They never speak to anybody, unless it's absolutely necessary, but everyone in Le Mourillon, as you know, goes his own way, and is never surprised at anything. The captain for one . . .'

"'What captain?'

"'Captain Gérard. It seems he is an ex-captain of Marines. Well, no one ever sees him . . . Sometimes when food has to be delivered at the house, and the lady is not in, some person shouts out an order from behind the door to leave the stuff on the step, and waits until you are a good distance away before taking it in.'

"You can imagine that I was growing more and more puzzled. I went to Toulon in order to ask the agent who let the villa a few questions about these people. He, likewise, had never seen the husband, but he told me that his name was Gérard Beauvisage.

"When I heard the name I uttered a cry: 'Gérard Beauvisage! Why I know him!'

"I had an old friend of that name whom I had not seen for twenty-five years. He was an officer in the Marines and had left Toulon for Tonkin about that period. How could I doubt that it was he? At all events, I had a straightforward reason for calling on him, that very evening, though he was expecting a visit from his friends, for it was the anniversary of the famous night. I made up my mind to renew my old friendship with him.

"When I got back to Le Mourillon I espied in front of me, in the sunken road leading to the Villa Makoko, the figure of my neighbour. I did not hesitate, but hastened to overtake her.

" 'Have I the honour of speaking to Madame Beauvisage, the wife of Captain Gérard Beauvisage?' I asked with a bow.

"She coloured and tried to pass on without answering me.

" 'Madame, I am your neighbour, Captain Michel Alban,' I persisted.

" 'Oh please forgive me, monsieur,' she returned, 'my husband has often spoken of you . . . Captain Michel Alban . . .'

"She seemed terribly ill at ease, and yet in her confusion she was more beautiful than ever, if that were possible. In spite of her obvious desire to elude me I went on:

" 'How comes it that Captain Beauvisage has returned to France without letting his old friend know? I shall be particularly obliged if you will tell Gérard that I'm coming to shake hands with him this very evening.'

"And observing that she was hastening her steps, I bowed, but as I was speaking she turned round, betraying an agitation which was more and more difficult to comprehend.

" 'Impossible tonight . . . I promise to tell Gérard of our meeting. That's the most I can do. Gérard doesn't wish to see anyone – anyone. He lives alone . . . We live alone . . . And we took the house because we were told that the next house was occupied only for a few days once or twice a year by someone who is never seen! . . .'

"And she added in a voice tinged with sadness:

" 'You must forgive Gérard, monsieur. We do not receive anyone – anyone. Good day, monsieur.'

" 'Madame, the Captain and you receive friends occasionally,' I returned with some impatience. 'For instance, tonight you are expecting friends with whom you made an appointment a year ago.'

"She flushed scarlet.

" 'Oh, but that's an exceptional case . . . that's an absolutely exceptional case . . . They are our very particular friends.'

"Having said which she made her escape, but at once stopped her retreat and turned back.

" 'Whatever you do, don't call tonight,' she entreated, and disappeared into the garden.

"I returned to my house and began to keep watch on my neighbours. They did not show themselves, and long before it was dark I saw the shutters being closed and lights gleaming through the openings, such as I had seen on that amazing night a year ago. But I did not hear the same extraordinary din like the thunderous beating of a wooden drum.

"At seven o'clock I began to dress for I called to mind the low-necked robe worn by the lady of the lamp. Madame Beauvisage's last words had but strengthened my determination. The captain was seeing some of his friends that evening; he dared not refuse me admission. After dressing it crossed my mind, before I went downstairs, to put my revolver in my pocket, but in the end I left it in its place, considering that to take it would be an act of stupidity.

"The stupidity lay in not taking it with me.

"On reaching the entrance to the Villa Makoko I turned the handle of the gate on the off chance – the handle which last year I had seen turn by itself. And to my intense surprise the door opened. Therefore my neighbours were expecting visitors. I walked up to the house and knocked at the door.

" 'Come in!' a voice cried.

"I recognised Gérard's voice. I walked gaily into the house. I passed first through the hall, and then as the door of a small drawing-room stood open, and the room was lit up, I entered it.

" 'Gérard, it's me,' I exclaimed, 'your old pal Michel Alban.'

" 'Oh, really, so you made up your mind to come, my dear old Michel! I told my wife only just now that you would come and I should be glad to see you . . . But you are the only one, apart from our particular friends . . . Do you know, my dear Michel, you haven't altered much . . .'

"It would be impossible for me to describe my stupefaction. I heard Gérard, but I could not see him. His voice rang in my ears, but no one was near me, no one was in the drawing-room. The Voice went on:

" 'Sit down, won't you? My wife will soon be here, for she will remember that she left me on the mantelpiece!'

"I looked up, and then discovered above me . . . above me resting on a high mantelpiece – a bust.

"It was this bust which had been speaking. It resembled Gérard. It was Gérard's body. It had been placed there as people are wont to place busts on mantelpieces. It was a bust like those carved by sculptors, that is to say, it was without arms.

" 'I can't shake hands with you, my dear Michel,' the Voice went on, 'for as you see I have no hands, but if you raise yourself on tiptoe you will be able to take me in your arms and place me on the table. My wife put me up here in a moment of temper, because she said I was in the way when she swept the room. She's a funny thing is my wife.'

"And the bust burst out laughing.

"It seemed to me that I was the victim of an optical illusion as happens in those entertainments where you behold living heads and shoulders suspended in mid-air, the result of tricks with mirrors; but after setting down my friend on the table, as he requested, I had to admit that this head and body without arms or legs was indeed all that remained of the excellent officer whom I had known in days gone by. His body was resting on a small wheeled platform, such as are used by cripples without legs, but Gérard did not possess even the stumps of most cripples. To think that my old friend was nothing but a bust!

"Small hooks took the place of arms, and language fails me to describe how, leaning for support on a hook here, or on another there, he set to work to hop, skip and jump and perform a hundred swift movements which shot him from the table to a chair, from a chair to the floor, and then suddenly made him appear on the table once more, where he indulged in the gayest chatter.

"Myself, I was in a state of consternation. I was rendered

speechless. I watched this freak perform his antics and say with a chuckle which alarmed me:

" 'I have greatly changed I daresay. You must admit, my dear Michel, that you hardly recognise me. You did quite right to call this evening. We shall see some sport. We have a few very special friends, and, you know, apart from them I don't care to meet anyone – merely as a matter of pride. We don't even keep a servant. Wait for me here. I must get into my smoking jacket.'

"He went off, and almost at once the lady of the lamp appeared. She wore the same low-necked dress of the year before. As soon as her eyes fell upon me, she seemed strangely perturbed, and said in a strained voice:

" 'Oh, so you are here! You've made a mistake, Captain Michel. I gave your message to my husband, but I forbade you to call this evening. I may tell you that when he learnt that you were in this place, he asked me to invite you this evening, but I did no such thing because,' she went on, ill at ease, 'I had good reasons. We have certain very particular friends who are rather a worry – they are very fond of noise – uproar. You must have heard them last year,' she added, giving me a look out of the corner of her eye. 'Well, promise me to leave early.'

" 'I promise to leave early, madame,' I returned, and yet a vague misgiving took possession of me at this conversation the meaning of which I was far from understanding. 'I promise you faithfully, but can you tell me how it is that I find my old friend in such a state? What terrible accident happened to him?'

" 'None at all, monsieur, none.'

" 'What do you mean, "none at all"? Don't you know anything about the accident which deprived him of arms and legs? Yet he must have met with it since your marriage.'

" 'No, monsieur, no. I married the captain as he is now . . . But excuse me, our guests will be here presently, and I must help my husband to put on his smoking jacket.'

"She left me to myself, dazed by the one stupefying thought: 'She married the captain as he is now!' and almost at once I heard sounds in the hall, the curious sounds which had accompanied the lady of the lamp to the garden gate and baffled me last year.

This noise was followed by the appearance, on their wheeled platforms, of four cripples without arms or legs who stared at me in wonder. They were all attired in perfectly-fitting evening dress with snow-white shirt fronts.

"One wore gold-rimmed pince-nez, another, an old man, spectacles, the third a single eye-glass, and the fourth was content to gaze at me out of his own proud, shrewd eyes with an expression of boredom. All four, however, saluted me with their little hooks, and asked after Captain Beauvisage. I told them that he was dressing, and Madame Beauvisage was quite well. When I took the liberty of speaking of Madame Beauvisage, I caught an exchange of glances between them which seemed to embody a certain raillery.

" 'Haw, haw, I presume you are a great friend of our good old captain,' drawled the cripple with the monocle.

"The others smiled with a look which was by no means pleasant, and then they all started to talk in the same breath:

" 'Sorry, sorry, monsieur . . . We are quite naturally surprised to meet you at the house of the good old captain, who swore on his wedding day to shut himself up in the country with his wife, and not to receive anyone – anyone but his very special friends, you understand. When one is so thoroughly a cripple as the captain consented to be, and is married to such a beautiful woman, it is quite natural – quite natural. But, after all, if in the course of his life he met a man of honour who does not happen to be a cripple, we're glad of it . . . We congratulate you.'

"And they repeated: 'We're glad of it . . . We congratulate you.'

"Lord, how odd they were, these dwarfs! I watched them and held my peace. Others arrived in twos and threes and so on. And they all contemplated me with a look of surprise or uneasiness or irony. For my part I was rendered speechless by the spectacle of so many cripples without arms or legs; for after all I was beginning to see through most of the extraordinary happenings which had so greatly stirred my mind; and though the cripples, by their presence, explained many things, the presence of the cripples still required explanation, as also did the monstrous union of that splendid woman with that awful shred of humanity.

"True, I realised now that these little ambulating trunks were bound to pass unperceived by me in the narrow garden path lined with verbena, and the road running between two low hedges; and, truth to tell, when at the time I said to myself that it was impossible to avoid seeing any person going down those paths, I had in mind persons who would be standing upright on their two legs.

"The handle of the garden gate itself no longer puzzled me, and in my mind's eye I saw the invisible hook which had turned it.

"The peculiar noise which I heard was but the creaking made by the small badly oiled wheels of these cars for freaks. Finally, the extraordinary sound like the thunderous beating of a wooden drum was obviously caused by the many cars and hooks striking the floor when, after an excellent dinner, our friends the cripples indulged in a dance.

"Yes all this was capable of explanation but I was conscious as I caught a curious eager gleam in their eyes, and heard the peculiar sound of their nippers, that something terrible still remained to be cleared up, and that all else which had surprised me was of no account.

"Meanwhile Madame Beauvisage promptly appeared, accompanied by her husband. They were greeted with shouts of delight. The little hooks 'applauded' them with an infernal din. I was deafened by it. Then I was introduced. Cripples were all over the place: on the tables, chairs, stools, on stands usually occupied by vases, on the sideboard. One of them sat on the shelf of a dresser like a Buddha in his recess. And each one politely held out his hook to me. They seemed for the most part people of good position, with titles and names indicating their relationship to aristocratic families, but I learned afterwards that these were false names given to me for reasons which will be obvious. Lord Wilmer certainly maintained the best front of them all, with his fine golden beard and no less fine moustache which he continually stroked with his hook. He did not leap from chair to table like the others, nor did he have the air of a huge bat taking wing from wall to wall.

" 'We are only waiting for the doctor,' said the mistress of the house, who every now and then gave me a look of obvious gloom, but quickly resumed her smile for her guests.

"The doctor arrived. He was a cripple but he possessed both arms.

"He offered one of them to Madame Beauvisage and led her to the dining-room. I mean that she touched his arm with the tips of her fingers.

"Covers were laid in the room with the closed shutters. The table, which was laden with flowers and *hors d'oeuvre*, was illuminated by a large candelabrum. There was no fruit. The dozen cripples at once leapt upon their chairs and began to pick greedily from the dishes with their hooks. It was not a pleasant sight, and I marvelled at the voracity with which these trunks of men, who seemed just before so well-mannered, devoured their food.

"And then suddenly they quietened down; their hooks kept still, and it seemed to me that they lapsed into what is usually described as a 'painful silence'.

"Every eye was turned on Madame Beauvisage, whose husband sat by her side, and I noticed that she buried her face in her napkin, looking very uncomfortable. Then my friend Gérard, clapping one hook against the other with a flourish, said:

" 'Well, my dear old friends, it can't be helped. One doesn't meet the luck of last year every day. But don't distress yourselves; with the exercise of a little imagination we shall succeed in being as merry as we were then . . .'

"And turning to me as he lifted the small handle of the glass which stood on the table before him:

" 'Your health, my dear Michel. To us all!'

"And each man raised his glass by its handle with the end of his hook. The glasses swung over the table in the quaintest fashion.

"My host went on:

" 'You don't seem to be equal to the occasion, my dear Michel.

I have known you in merrier mood, more up to the mark. Is it because we are "like this" that you are so gloomy? What do you expect? We are what we are. But let us have some amusement. We are met together here, all of us very special friends, to celebrate the time when we became "like this". Is that not true my friends of the *Daphné*? . . .'

"Then my old comrade," Captain Michel went on to explain, heaving a deep sigh, "told us how the *Daphné*, which sailed between France and the Far East, was wrecked; how the crew escaped in the boats, and how these miserable people took refuge on a chance raft.

"Miss Madge, a beautiful young girl who lost her parents in the catastrophe, was also picked up by the raft. Some thirteen persons in all were on it, and at the end of three days the victuals were consumed, and at the end of a week the survivors were dying of hunger. It was then that, as the old song says, they agreed to draw lots as to 'which should be eaten'.

"Messieurs," added Captain Michel, in a serious voice, "such things have happened more often perhaps than they have been talked about, for the great blue waters close over these peculiar feats of digestion.

"They were on the point, therefore, of drawing lots on the raft when the doctor's voice was heard: 'Mesdames and Messieurs,' said the doctor, 'you have lost all your belongings in the wreck of the ship, but I have saved my case of instruments and my forceps for arresting haemorrhage. This is my suggestion: There is no object in any one of us running the risk of being eaten as a whole. Let us, to begin with, draw lots for an arm or leg at will, and we will then see tomorrow what the day brings forth, and perhaps a sail may appear on the horizon.' "

At this point in Captain Michel's story the four old salts, who up to this had not interrupted, cried:

"Well done!"

"What do you mean 'well done'?" asked Captain Michel with a frown.

"Yes, 'well done'! Your story is a good joke. These people

were ready to lose an arm or leg in turn . . . That's a good joke, but there's nothing frightful about it."

"So you really find it a good joke!" growled the Captain, bristling with annoyance. "Well, I swear that if you had been seated among all those cripples whose eyes were bulging like live coal, and heard the story, you wouldn't have found it such a good joke . . . And if you had noticed how restless they were in their chairs! And how vigorously they clasped hooks across the table with an obvious delight which I couldn't make out, but which was none the less frightful for all that."

"No, no," broke in Chaulieu once more – that old fellow Chaulieu – "your story is not in the least frightful. It is funny simply because it is logical. Would you like me to tell you the end of the story? You shall say whether I am right or not. The people on the raft drew lots. The lot fell to Miss Madge who was to lose one of her beautiful limbs. Your friend the captain, who is a gentleman, offered his own instead, and he had his four limbs amputated so that Miss Madge should remain unscathed."

"Yes, old man, you've got it. That is so," exclaimed Captain Michel who felt a longing to break the heads of these imbeciles who treated his story as a good joke. "Yes, and what's more, when it was a question of cutting off Miss Madge's limbs after the survivors, except the young lady and the doctor – who had been left with both arms because they were wanted – had lost all their limbs, Captain Beauvisage had the pluck to have the poor stumps left from the first operation, cut off on a level with his body."

"And the young lady could do no other than offer the Captain her hand which he had so heroically saved," interposed Zinzin.

"Why, of course," growled the Captain in his beard. "And you consider it a good joke!"

"Did they eat all those limbs quite raw?" enquired that ass of a Bagatelle.

Captain Michel struck the table such a resounding blow that the glasses danced like rubber balls.

"That'll do, shut up," he exclaimed. "All that I've told you is nothing. Now comes the frightful part of it."

The four friends looked at each other smiling, and Captain

Michel grew pale, whereupon seeing that they had carried matters too far they hung their heads.

"Yes, the frightful part of it," went on Michel with his gloomiest air, "was that these people who were only rescued a month later by a Chinese sailing vessel which landed them somewhere on the Yang-Tse-Kiang where they separated – the frightful part of it was that these people retained a taste for human flesh, and when they returned to Europe arranged to meet together once a year to renew as far as possible the abominable banquet. Well, messieurs, it did not take me long to find that out! First of all there was the scarcely enthusiastic reception accorded to certain dishes, which Madame Beauvisage herself brought to the table. Though she ventured to claim, but with no great assurance, that they were pretty nearly the same thing, the guests were of one mind in abstaining from congratulating her. Only certain slices of tunny-fish were received with any sort of favour, because they were, to use the doctor's terrible expression, 'well cut', and, 'if the flavour was not entirely satisfactory at all events the eye was deceived'. But the cripple with the spectacles met with general approval when he declared that 'it was not equal to the plumber'.

"When I heard those words I felt my blood run cold," growled Captain Michel huskily, "for I remembered that about this time the year before a plumber had fallen from a roof near the Arsenal and was killed, and his body was picked up minus an arm.

"Then . . . O then . . . I could not help thinking of the part which my beautiful neighbour must, of necessity, have played in this horrible, culinary drama. I turned my eyes to her and I noticed that she had put on her gloves again, gloves which covered her arms to the shoulder, and also hastily thrown a wrap over her shoulders which wholly concealed them. The guest on my right, who was the doctor, and, as I have said, was the only man among the cripples with both arms intact, had also put on his gloves.

"Instead of bothering my head in vain to discover the reason of this fresh eccentricity, I should have done better to follow the advice which Madame Beauvisage gave me at the beginning of this infernal party, namely, to leave the place early—advice which she did not repeat.

"After showing an interest in me during the first part of this amazing feast in which I seemed to discern—I don't know why—a sort of pity, Madame Beauvisage now avoided looking at me and took a part which greatly grieved me in the most frightful conversation which I have ever heard. These little people with a vigorous clatter of nippers and clinking of glasses indulged in bitter recriminations or warm congratulations with regard to their peculiar appetite.

"To my horror Lord Wilmer who until then had been most correct, nearly 'came to hooks' with the cripple with the monocle, because the latter had once on the raft complained of the former being tough, and the mistress of the house had the greatest difficulty in putting things in their true light by retorting to the monocled bust, who was obviously at the time of the shipwreck a good-looking stripling, that neither was it particularly agreeable to have to put up with 'an animal that was too young'."

"That's also funny," the old salt Dorat could not help interjecting.

It looked as if Captain Michel would fly at his throat, particularly as the three other mariners seemed to be shaking with inward joy and gave vent to queer little clucks. It was as much as the Captain could do to control himself. After puffing like a seal he turned to the foolhardy Dorat:

"Monsieur, you have two arms still, and I have no wish for you to lose one of them, as I did on that particular night, to make you see the frightful part of the story. The cripples had drunk a great deal. Some of them jumped on the table round me, and were gazing at my arms in a very embarrassing manner and I ended by hiding them from sight as far as possible by thrusting my hands deep into my pockets.

"I realised then, and it was a startling thought, why Madame Beauvisage and the doctor, the two persons who still had arms and hands, did not show them. I grasped the meaning of the sudden ferocity which blazed in the eyes of some of them. And at that very moment, as luck would have it, I wanted to use my pocket handkerchief, and instinctively I made a movement which revealed the whiteness of my skin under my sleeve, and three terrible hooks swooped down at once on my wrist and entered my flesh. I uttered a fearful shriek."

"That'll do, Captain, that'll do," I exclaimed, interrupting Captain Michel's story. "You were quite right. I'm off. I can't stand any more."

"Stay, monsieur," said the Captain in a peremptory tone. "Stay, monsieur, for I shall soon finish this frightful story which has made four imbeciles laugh. When a man has Phocean blood in his veins," he added with an accent of unspeakable contempt turning to the four ancient mariners who were obviously choking in their efforts to keep back their laughter, "when a man has Phocean blood in his veins, he can't get over it.

"And when a man lives in Marseilles he is doomed never to believe in anything. So it is for you, for you alone, monsieur, that I am telling this story, and, be assured, I will pass over the most loathsome details, knowing as I do how much the mind of a gentleman can bear. The tragedy of my martyrdom proceeded so quickly that I can call to mind only their inhuman cries, the protests of some and the rush of others while Madame Beauvisage stood up and murmured:

" 'Be careful not to hurt him!'

"I tried to leap to my feet, but by this time a posse of mad cripples was round me who tripped me up and I crashed to the floor. And I felt their awful hooks hold my flesh captive just as the meat in a butcher's shop is held captive on its hooks.

"Yes, monsieur, I will spare you the details. I pledged you my word; all the more so as I couldn't give them to you, for I did not see the operation. The doctor clapped a plug of cotton wool steeped in chloroform on my mouth by way of a gag.

"When I came to myself I was in the kitchen, and I had lost an arm. The cripples were all around me. They had ceased their wrangling. They seemed to be united in the most touching harmony; in reality they were in a state of dazed intoxication which caused them to sway their heads like children who feel the need to go and lie down after eating their fill, and I had not a doubt but that they were beginning, alas! to digest me . . . I was stretched at full length on the floor, securely bound, and deprived of all power of movement, but I could both see and hear them. My old comrade, Gérard Beauvisage, had tears of joy in his eyes as he exclaimed:

" 'I should never have thought you would be so tender!'

"Madame Beauvisage was not present, but she, too, must have taken part in the feast, for I heard someone ask Gérard how 'she liked her share'.

"Yes, monsieur, I have finished my story. I have finished my story. Those loathsome cripples having satisfied their weakness, must have at last realised the full extent of their iniquity. They made themselves scarce, and Madame Beauvisage, of course, escaped with them. They left the doors wide open but no one came to set me free until four days afterwards, when I was pretty well dead with hunger . . .

"Those miserable wretches had not even left the bone behind!"

THE MYSTERY OF THE FOUR HUSBANDS

THE OLD SEA-DOGS who spent their evenings seated on the terrace of the inn which overlooked the sea had never seen Zinzin arrive in such a condition before. His eyes were popping from his head, and he was as pale as death. As soon as he had had time to drop into a chair, they pressed anxiously around him.

"What is the matter, Zinzin? What is the matter, old fellow?" Captain Michel asked.

Zinzin made a sign that he was still unable to speak, but at last he wiped his forehead.

"I have just come from the police commissioner," he began, "and he gave me a most horrible bit of news."

"Tell us about it before it becomes old stuff," Gobert exclaimed. "The story is sure to change with time."

"Oh, this doesn't date from yesterday," Zinzin murmured with a sinister laugh.

"Then why so much excitement today?"

"I'll tell you why shortly," the other replied dismally. "I was mixed up in it when I was very young. It narrowly missed making me a landlubber forever with a little garden plot over me! On my word! It's not the fault of the damned wedding story if I'm not fertilising a crop of dandelions today. It caused a lot of stir in its time. They even took the case up to the court of assizes!"

"Stories of marriages exist by the legion," grouchy old Chaulieu remarked. "I know ten myself."

"I only know one," Zinzin replied with a groan, "but I warn you that it is more horrible than all ten of Chaulieu's put together!"

He sighed heavily again and lighted his pipe. "I never told you anything about it before," he spat out, "because it seemed such an utterly fantastic affair, but today I must talk! Good God! Good God!"

"Well, what is it? What is it, Zinzin?"

"It is a horrible story," Zinzin choked.

"Perhaps," Chaulieu added quietly and sceptically.

Zinzin cast him a murderous look. "In all my life I have only been in love once," he went on, "and it was that time. It never happened again because I never met another such girl. Her name was Olympe, and there were a dozen of us who wanted to marry her."

"And here the impossible begins," sneered Chaulieu.

"Twelve, I tell you! I'll give you their names in a moment, and that doesn't include those who did not openly propose. There wasn't a man in the whole country who would not have wanted to. She wasn't rich, but she came of good family – and beautiful! At the time of which I speak she was just seventeen years old. Her section of the country was noted for its beautiful women – a big pleasant suburb worth visiting if only to watch the girls come home from church on Sundays.

"Well! In all the town there was not one girl fit to tie her shoes, and that meant a lot . . . Listen, if you have ever gone to Cagnes, perhaps you have seen Renoir's portraits of young girls . . . Those pictures are pure fantasy – pictures of flowers and sunlight, not humans. Well, Olympe was like that: a ray of sun and the petals of a rose. A dream! But a dream with eyes and a mouth! . . . enormous childish eyes with supernatural purity in their gaze, and the mouth of a woman! The mouth alone was of flesh and blood! Olympe was like an angel come down to earth to kiss!

"We were all crazy about her. She lived alone with her grandmother, who had taken her from school at the death of her parents and entrusted her to the safe care of the servant Palmire, who was the girl's willing slave. Olympe was still much of a child, often playing with the country urchins, returning home with armfuls of wild flowers, baskets filled with wild strawberries. She would run behind the flocks with the sheepdogs when she crossed them on the road, and often scandalised the old women by returning home at night astride a goat!

"In nice weather the old people would sit outside their doors on little wooden benches and wait for her to come. She had a wonderful imagination and told them stories which she made up as she went along.

"The grandmother, who in her day had been the beautiful Madame Gratien, lived in a big old house on the Place de l'Abbaye. The gardens were closed in by walls and at the back looked out on the open country. She knew all the élite of the neighbourhood and had maintained connections in the city.

"The behaviour of her granddaughter had amused her in the beginning but at last it began to preoccupy her. Olympe seemed very thoughtless for her age . . . What would happen when she was alone in the world? Madame Gratien suddenly decided to marry her off as soon as possible.

"She had already received several offers for the hand of her granddaughter, and when it was known that she no longer discouraged suitors, they besieged her on all sides. This flood of admirers was a new game for Olympe. Finally one Sunday we were all gathered in the living-room, when the grandmother gave Olympe a little talking-to. She told her that she was beginning to be very tired and weary with life and that she would like to see Olympe settled down before she died. Olympe greeted this announcement with tears. We thought that the prospect of the old lady's death saddened her, but Olympe explained it differently. 'As though it were gay to marry!' she said when we tried to cheer her up.

"We burst out laughing at that and all swore that her husband would be perfectly willing to be her slave.

" 'First of all, I do not want to leave Grandmother,' she said, 'nor Palmire . . . And secondly I want to live in our old house.'

" 'Agreed, agreed,' we answered in chorus.

" 'And now,' said good Madame Gratien, 'which one are you going to choose?'

" 'Oh, we'll talk of that later,' said Olympe. 'This is no way to marry people off. You're really not serious about it, Grandmother!'

" 'For six months you've said the same thing: that you'd talk it over later. Now, it's become a joke. You know that I have always

done everything you wanted before . . . Come; if you were obliged to choose one of these gentlemen, which would you take?'

"Olympe suddenly became serious, and we watched her
anxiously . . . In spite of our apparent acceptance of the whole
thing as a joke, we were deadly serious . . .

"She stood up, walked around us, and sized us up from head to
foot with such funny expressions that we were more than a little
embarrassed. If I live to be a thousand, I'll never forget that
scene! What an examination! To be truthful, we hardly dared
breathe.

"She made us stand, lined us up, placing us, changing us – ad-
vancing a man to the head of the line and then, after looking him
straight in the eyes, sending him back to third or fourth position.
The grandmother encouraged us from time to time with a 'Hold
yourselves well, gentlemen! . . . Hold yourselves well! . . . Be
serious.'

"It was funny when one thinks that we were not all young men
either! I well remember the arrival of the town registrar, respectable Monsieur Pacifire, who for two years had openly bid for
Olympe's hand. He came late and naturally did not know what it
was all about.

"She met him at the door and placed him, dumbfounded, at
the end of the line. He had the last number! You can imagine
how we laughed. But you can bet that when he knew what it was
all about, he did not laugh at all!

" 'At last! It is done!' she announced. 'If I marry I'll take
Monsieur Delphin *first*, then Monsieur Hubert, then Monsieur
Sabin, then my little Zinzin (as you see, I was number four), then
Monsieur Jacobini . . .' and she went on down the whole twelve
of us . . . I'll enumerate them: 1st, Monsieur Delphin, a nice
fellow with a great future ahead of him, son of the town pharmac-
ist; he had taken his degree in science, was working for a fellowship in chemistry and was very well spoken of at the university.
2nd Monsieur Hubert, still young, about twenty-five, head forest
warden. 3rd, Dr Felix Sabin, just out of college, and as merry as a
lark . . . I think he had settled himself in the country with the
idea of getting into politics. 4th, yours truly, who had already

taken to the sea but who would have given it all up to stay with Olympe. 5th, Lieutenant Jacobini, son of a colonel in the guards, a distinguished, smart fellow who had just come back from a mission in South Africa where he had made something of a name for himself. 6th, the son of a big landowner with lots of money. 7th, a young lawyer. 8th, the son of a solicitor. 9th, an old notary. 10th, a travelling salesman. 11th, the assistant of the district attorney. 12th, Monsieur Pacifire, the registrar ... yes, that makes twelve. We were only twelve that day!

"Six months later, Olympe married number one, young Delphin. We all went to the wedding – but not to have a good time. I tried to reason against it, but I would have given anything to be in Delphin's shoes. The following year, however, I no longer envied him. He was dead!

"No one knows exactly what he died of. They say that he was poisoned by some laboratory work, but nothing was sure. The physician who attended him, Dr Sabin, shook his head when he was questioned. I think that in reality he thought of only one thing, in short, that he had now become number two and that if anything were to happen to the forest warden who preceded him, he might yet hope for a chance!

"It seemed impossible, but Olympe had become even lovelier since her marriage. Now, when she passed in her widow's weeds, she was something to kneel before and worship. But she did not mourn her dead husband for long. In fact, if one can believe old Palmire, Monsieur Delphin was not excessively gay and for a young husband spent too much time in his laboratories, leaving his young wife for entire days while he searched for heaven knows what in the bottoms of his test-tubes.

"Monsieur Hubert's turn was bound to arrive, and he did not lose time in pressing his suit and in promising her all the gaieties that she had missed since her first marriage. He was a jolly fellow, that Hubert, fond of good food, an excellent drinker and hunter as was fitting with a man of his position and name.

"Big celebrations and big parties now took place at Olympe's. She began to ride horseback and there was not another like her for fifty miles around. It was a sight to see her hunt the deer and wild boar. Nothing frightened her. We had trouble to keep up with her, and afterwards she presided over the banquet with a sparkle and an ardour that gave us all fever.

"She was more courted than ever, but she made fun of us, and kept her loveliest and gayest smiles for Dr Sabin. 'He is number three,' she exclaimed, laughing. 'Everyone in turn!'

" 'Hey!' Hubert interrupted. 'I never felt better in my life!'

" 'And I take care of him,' replied the doctor. 'He is the one man whom I'm not permitted to kill. Thank the fortune, Hubert, which prohibits me from choosing my victims!'

"This was all very nice, but it seemed to me that Dr Sabin made too much use of his position of family doctor in order to be familiar with Olympe. They were often seen alone in the park behind the house, or even going for a little outing in the forest when Hubert, called away on business or some bachelor party in the neighbouring town, left Olympe for a few hours. She had become the general topic of conversation in the village. She scandalised the habitués of the five o'clock teas at Madame Tabureau's, the mayor's wife, or at Madame Blancmougin's, the wife of the solicitor whose son had received number eight in the general classing. Madame Blancmougin never ceased congratulating herself on her son's lucky escape.

"In fact, after the death of old Madame Gratien, which had occurred in the meantime, Olympe no longer kept her desires within any limits and she frightened many people by the liberty of those desires. Hubert made no attempt to restrain her. He was amused and flattered by the number of victims won by those innocent blue eyes and that bright mouth which seemed to be always asking for a kiss.

"He was a good liver, that Hubert, but not a real lover. 'My!' Palmire would whisper to those who liked to be informed of all that went on in the house, 'he certainly loves his food more than his bed. If Madame were not so honest, that fact might give him a bad jolt!'

"And so saying, she shook her head on seeing Olympe and Dr

Sabin come in from one of the lessons in driving. Those driving lessons had started a lot of gossip which was cut short by a new misfortune in Place de l'Abbaye.

"Delphin had installed a laboratory in an isolated building in a far corner of the grounds and this Hubert had made into a sort of hunting-pavilion. He had furnished it with his guns, his knives, his rifles, his pistols, and had also stored his ammunition there. It was like a little armoury, with the exception of the walls, which were decorated with the usual trophies. It was a pleasant little spot, covered with climbing vines and flowers, and there was a fine view of the fields and country beyond. He often had lunch served there in order to be alone with his wife or friends away from the ears of the servants.

"It was there that Hubert was found one afternoon in August with a pistol in his hands and a bullet through his heart.

"Suicide or accident? Several even murmured the word: crime! . . . but it was said so low that no one heard them.

"You can imagine what a stir it caused. An inquest was held. The assistant district attorney, who was number eleven, managed the affair. It was Dr Sabin, number three, who was called to give his opinion on the nature of the death. He pronounced it accident. The inquest hesitated a long time between accident and suicide, but they finally concluded with the theory of the accident.

" 'My goodness!' Palmire sighed when she was besieged by many wanting to know what Madame had to say about the death of her husband. 'What should she say? She knew nothing about it, of course. She had lunched in the little pavilion with Monsieur . . . They both had seemed very gay. She left him at about two-thirty in order to dress, for she was going to town with Dr Sabin. About three o'clock the gardener heard a shot and ran to the pavilion. He found Monsieur stretched out dead. And now you know as much as we do. Why should he have committed suicide? Life was beautiful and so was Olympe. He had every-thing to make him happy. And now Olympe is crying her eyes out, which is a stupid thing to do. No one is responsible for an accident, and it was his fault for not being more careful!'

"So spoke Palmire. The next year Olympe married Dr Sabin."

"I expected it," interrupted Chaulieu; "if your blue-eyed angel with the passionate mouth had to give herself to all twelve of those gentlemen we haven't finished and it's not going to be a funny tale."

"I didn't promise you a funny story. I told you that it was horrible. Olympe did not give herself to all twelve, since I was number four and I'm still alive. Nevertheless, I excuse Chaulieu for his remark because in the village they began to say: 'They'll all go. She's capable of it.'

" 'And why not? If it pleases Olympe?' Palmire replied whenever she heard something of that kind. And she added, scratching her long chin, 'She would be wrong in hesitating over it as far as the worth of those men is concerned!'

"It was a terrible thing that she said, in the ignorance of a servant ready to perjure her soul for her mistress.

"Dr Sabin was certainly a courageous fellow to marry into a household which seemed destined to misfortune. Some good old woman of the kind particularly skilful in slipping in a malicious remark between a frown and a smile, remarked, however, 'Oh, nothing will happen to *him*. He knows what he is doing!'

"The town was a-buzz with horrible remarks. Poor doctor! He did not deserve what was said, since he, too, died, exactly three months to the day after his wedding. He lasted even a shorter time than the others."

"Good Lord!" Gaubert whistled.

"And so it came your turn," said Captain Michel.

"It's beginning to be very amusing," remarked Chaulieu.

But they all stopped joking. Zinzin had become terribly pale and his hand trembled as he put down his glass. He looked with wild eyes at a man who was approaching the table.

"Hello," exclaimed the captain, "here's the police commissioner's orderly."

It was he in fact, and he bent over and whispered in Zinzin's ear:

"We've just had a telephone message. She has been dead ten

years. You don't need to worry any longer." And with that he departed.

As for Zinzin, he staggered into the captain's arms and had to be taken home.

"Let's hope he doesn't kick off before the end of his story," said Gaubert gently.

Chaulieu shrugged his shoulders. "Bah," he said, "he is working for a climactic effect."

Nevertheless we did not know the end of the story until eight days later. Zinzin certainly had been very ill. This time we listened without interrupting him.

"It was my turn then, number four's turn. But I was still ignorant of the fact. I was sailing in the Baltic Sea when the thing happened, and I did not learn it until my return ashore. I threw myself on a train for home and on the way met Lieutenant Jacobini, number five, who had himself returned only a short while ago.

"Our trip was not a merry one. I confess that in spite of the certainty I now had of being able to marry Olympe and in spite of the hope Lieutenant Jacobini had of soon being able to cheer up my widow, this double prospect did not fill us with merriment. The house on Place de l'Abbaye seemed less like a place of joy to us now and more like a tomb!

"The first thing I asked Jacobini, after he had told me the sinister news, was naturally if he could give me a few details on the doctor's death. How had he died? He answered gloomily that he hadn't the faintest idea and that no one else had either; but that he more than anyone wanted to get to the bottom of it. That was the reason for his return.

" 'And you?' he asked me.

" 'Oh,' I answered, 'as for me, you can understand that I am interested in the matter at least as much as you are.'

" 'Yes,' he replied without the slightest sarcasm, 'I understand that . . . It is an even more urgent matter for you.'

" 'But,' I went on, 'they must have called his death by some name!'

" 'Not any more of a name than they gave the death of Olympe's first husband. They claimed that Delphin was poisoned by some laboratory experiment, but the thing was never proved. And as far as Dr Sabin is concerned it can't be that.'

" 'All these deaths are certainly very strange! Tell me, Jacobini, aren't the police interested in this?'

" 'Yes. Our assistant district attorney, number eleven, has ordered an investigation. I ought to add that Olympe was the first to ask it . . . They made an autopsy on the body . . .'

" 'And?'

" 'And found nothing . . . But that doesn't prove a thing,' he added in a tone which struck me.

" 'What do you mean? Have you a suspicion?'

" 'In such matters,' replied Jacobini, 'it is not permissible to have suspicions. One must be certain or keep still.' And he kept still.

"But all this did not tend to quiet my anxiety.

" 'Then he died in his bed? Was he ill?'

" 'No! Olympe found him about five o'clock in the afternoon in his room, stretched out on the floor with a table and chair overturned, his mouth still foaming and his face distorted from horror . . . It was proved that he had been in the room alone from three o'clock on and that the house was completely deserted, as the servants had gone to a nearby fair.'

" 'And – Madame Sabin?'

" 'She had lunched with him in the little pavilion at the end of the garden and had remained there to embroider with Palmire.'

" 'Then what was the conclusion of the inquest?'

" 'That Dr Sabin died from an attack of epilepsy.'

" 'Was he subject to it?'

" 'No, but it seems that that does not always follow.'

"We were silent a long time. Then I sighed.

" 'We ought to be sincerely sorry for Olympe,' I said, 'because otherwise it would be too horrible.'

" 'Yes,' he replied after thinking a moment, 'you are right! It would be too horrible . . . She must be pitied. Besides, Palmire says that she is completely crushed. No one ever sees her now.

She never goes out. According to gossip she wants to enter a convent . . . It is natural enough that after three unfortunate marriages like these she should be sick of matrimony – and – and I congratulate you,' he added with a strange laugh. Then he went on quickly, because he was an extremely polite fellow: 'I hope I haven't pained you in saying that?'

" 'I don't know,' I answered.

"We arrived an hour later. We hadn't forewarned anyone and it was already late at night. We had decided to go directly to the Hotel de Bourgogne, and I was surprised to find the solicitor's son, number eight, waiting for us on the platform. I remember his name now; he was called Juste. There is nothing to say about him except that he was an honest fellow, and that Dr Sabin had often treated him for rheumatism.

" 'I knew that you had landed,' he said to me, 'and that you were taking this train. What hotel are you going to?'

" 'To the Bourgogne with Lieutenant Jacobini.'

"Juste had been so preoccupied with me that he hadn't noticed my companion. He shook him warmly by the hand and said that he would go with us.

"I was growing more puzzled every moment. At the hotel he followed me to my room and gave me a packet for which he asked a receipt.

" 'This was entrusted to my honour,' he said, 'with the mission of giving it into your own hands.'

"I examined the sealed envelope quickly and recognised the writing immediately. My name was written on the outside with the addition: 'To be delivered after my death.'

" 'Yes,' the other replied, 'I have accomplished my mission and I am only accountable to him; but since I haven't the faintest idea of what is contained in that letter, I want a receipt, to be on the safe side.'

"I gave him his receipt.

" 'In giving you this letter,' I asked, 'Dr Sabin said nothing special?'

" 'Not a thing,' he replied. 'He told me nothing, absolutely nothing.'

"Upon which he shook my hand and took leave of me a bit hurriedly. He seemed free of a great weight. I opened the letter feverishly.

"Ten minutes later someone knocked at Jacobini's door. He was just about to get into bed and called out, asking who was there. As no one answered him, he went to the door and opened it impatiently. A ghost with a letter in its hands entered his room. This ghost was I and I hadn't strength enough even to speak. He sat me down, took the letter from my hands, locked the door and read.

"I will never forget him as he stood there, bent over the lamp. The letter which had plunged me into a sort of prostration had an entirely different effect on him. Everything about him seemed to tighten up while with me there had been a complete loosening of my willpower. He frowned heavily, his eyebrows were knitted, his chin grew more prominent, and a dangerous flame like the cold steel flash of a sword lit the eyes intent on reading the document, a document which had been written by the trembling hand of a man who knew himself condemned to death.

"This is what Dr Sabin had written. The original has long been in the police files but this is a copy:"

Dear Zinzin:

Before marrying Olympe I want you to read this: It is a man who is about to die who is writing to you. I have been horribly poisoned. No one knows it except the guilty one or guilty ones and me. I have not complained, for I have got only what I deserved. Thanks to strong drugs I have been able at times to overcome the pain which is destroying me and still to appear human. Thus I have been able to see Juste without giving anything away to him, nor will you tell him anything unless he, too, should want to marry Olympe – in which case you will show him this letter. But I hope that this will be the end of the matter and that after my death no one will wish to take my place, our place, the place of the three men who have entered this house full of health and life and who have disappeared from it, carrying with them the enigma of their triple misfortune.

As far as possible keep scandal from Olympe. I have loved her too much. I still love her, perhaps. No scandal, therefore, unless it be absolutely necessary. And besides, I am certain of nothing. In such a case, proof of the guilt is necessary, and I have none. I might be able to accuse her with a chance of not making a mistake, but I haven't the right; and I will tell you why. You know that after Hubert's death I returned a verdict of suicide. But Hubert did not commit suicide. Hubert was murdered!

And I knew the truth at my first sight of the body by the position of the pistol in his hand. The weapon had been placed in his hand, after his death! I won't go into details, but I could have proved it very easily. I had been called immediately after the discovery of the body in the hope that perhaps life still stirred within him, but it was all over. Next to the corpse stood Olympe in tears. Before looking at the woman I had seen the pistol and had already reached a conclusion. Then I looked at the woman. You may have suspected the affectionate ties that bound us already. Besides, Olympe made no effort to hide the truth, and I had spoken to her about it more than once. Looking at her, it seemed to me that her eyes wavered after catching mine and they left me the impression of an ardent and silent plea. Even today I am sure that I was not mistaken and I feel a chill of horror. That woman killed Hubert in order to be mine! It was horrible, but I adored her, and not only did I not denounce her, but without her noticing and for pity of her I slipped the pistol into the correct position. I made the matter easy for the board of experts. You see, Zinzin, old man, I'm not hiding anything from you. You understand now why I haven't the right to accuse this woman. My cowardice has made me her accomplice.

I think we loved each other like the damned, trying to forget in the embrace of love a lost paradise. Between us there never came a thought of Hubert or of Delphin. One would have said that Olympe had never known those two men. But I, I was curious to know how Delphin had died and I began a cunning investigation which one day they must have noticed. From that day on, I am sure, my death was decided.

Certain contradictory remarks made by Palmire concerning Delphin's experiments and the rather mysterious circumstances of his death led me to certain clues in which I found the almost certainty of Olympe's guilt in the poisoning of Delphin with Palmire as an accomplice. I had not said anything yet to Olympe, who did not seem to suspect my thoughts. I attempted to keep as hidden as possible the hideous suspicions. But one day I felt that I had been struck! A high fever, a strange uneasiness and dull pains warned me that I had been poisoned. I still said nothing because I wanted to know – to know. And I believed that I had done the necessary things to save me in time from a drug which was already attacking the sources of life – and which I could not rid myself of.

How did they go about it? . . . To make sure that it was she, I ate nothing except what she gave me, and we drank from the same glass. Yes, but we did not eat from the same plate! Ah, what horror! . . . And this is where the matter rests today as I write you this letter . . . I have just had an attack which I have concealed from her. Is she really ignorant of it? Or does she find pleasure in it? Lord God! And yet my face has changed in these last weeks and several times I have pushed her from my arms. Still she seems to have noticed nothing. Oh, the monster! The two monsters! Yes, two, because I have discovered Palmire spying on me and the two of them are always together. Nevertheless, Olympe said to me yesterday: "It's funny how men change after a few weeks of marriage! After a short while they are unrecognisable. They are no longer interesting!"

Zinzin, you will have this letter and I am going to talk to her. But I won't be telling her anything she doesn't already know. She must believe by now that I know by whose hands her first two husbands were killed; but I must tell her that I know that she is killing the third and that she must stop there!

Ah, Olympe, our Olympe! . . . If you knew, Zinzin, you

would understand – and you would pardon me . . . Perhaps, after all, she is not guilty – perhaps Palmire is responsible, perhaps Palmire did it all alone. Ah, my God, if that could be true! . . . This is an idea which has come to me a little late – too late! . . . Think it over, Zinzin. I am past thinking now. I suffer too much . . . And yet I do not like to die without knowing. If she could only prove to me that it is Palmire who did it alone! I love her still, Zinzin!

"After this last line the writing was so disordered and jumbled that it was difficult to read, and the signature which followed seemed to express the supreme effort of a man from whom life is escaping. And yet Dr Sabin could not have died that day. Probably by the feverish use of some medicine he was able to suspend his destiny. We know that the unfortunate man did not die until after lunch the next day . . .

"I made the copy which you have just read," Zinzin continued, "that same night, because Lieutenant Jacobini demanded the original. He had the right to it, *since he was going to take my place!* I said all the things that you or anyone would say in such horrible circumstances; but I realised that his mind was made up and that there was nothing more to do. Of course, it was no longer a question of love for Olympe.

"He had made a vow, a vow to punish her for her crimes. He would force her to confess, make her give herself up, and then we would see! . . .

"He did not tell me what we would see, but it was easy enough to understand on catching sight of his fierce, terrible look when he spoke.

" 'Dr Sabin got his just deserts,' he said to me, 'and I do not pity him; but that poor Hubert was my friend, and Delphin I loved as a younger brother and *I may be responsible for his death*. Therefore, I, Jacobini, am going to avenge them.'

"To accomplish that he decided to marry Olympe.

" 'And if she doesn't want to marry?' I asked him.

"He laughed a horrible laugh. 'A woman like her will not refuse a man like me!'

"He was right. Olympe married number five and I was best man for Jacobini. He insisted upon it. During the ceremony he stood with his arms crossed at the foot of the chancel beside his kneeling bride and looked already like a statue of vengeance. Olympe was no longer the girl we had all known and loved. There was something strangely funereal in her beauty and it seemed already to be bending under the hand of death. She looked like the figures in marble one sees on tombstones. I never expected to see her again, for the next day I set out to sea.

"At every port I threw myself on the newspapers; I opened my mail with trembling, feverish hands. No news reached me of the hideous tragedy that I felt must have been happening at home during my absence. When, three months later, I returned, my first question was . . . yes, you have guessed it . . .

" 'Is nothing changed around here?'

" 'Goodness, no.'

" 'And how are the Jacobinis?'

" 'The Jacobinis are fine,' I was told.

"The next day Jacobini came to call on me. He knew that I had just returned. He looked exceedingly well and had prolonged his furlough, since Olympe refused to leave the house even though he hated it. 'At heart I can't blame her,' he explained. 'She believes that if she leaves the house and this town where she spent such a happy youth it will look as though the evil tongues which claim she had a hand in the death of her three husbands have some cause for their suspicions.'

"I looked at Jacobini, but he met my gaze clearly.

" 'I understand your astonishment,' he said, 'but Olympe is not to be suspected.'

" 'So much the better, so much the better. Let's drop the subject, then.'

" 'Zinzin!'

" 'Yes, Jacobini!'

" 'I have come to talk to you and you must listen to me. The first thing I did on returning to the house after the wedding was to show her Dr Sabin's letter. Olympe cried, but did not seem in the least astonished.

" ' "I had a suspicion of that," she confessed to me. "Everybody thinks I am a monster. I wonder that you wanted to marry me."

" ' "I will tell you why in due time," I replied, "but for the moment we are concerned with Dr Sabin's letter."

" ' "What can I say?" she continued bitterly. "I am no more guilty of Hubert's death, of which they suspect me, than I am of my first husband's. Sabin loved me madly, and there were moments when his love was strangely like hatred. He let drop words from time to time that made me understand his horrible thought . . . and he started an abominable investigation. He questioned Palmire, who repeated everything to me. I tried to quiet him. Above all I wanted to avoid any scandal. I told myself that his state of mind would pass with time and that as I had nothing to hide, he would end by understanding that we were all the victims of a horrible fate. Then suddenly he believed himself poisoned. He did not tell me in the beginning. I myself did not mention the word 'poison', so that nothing definite should happen between us. I did not want to be forced to call in the police or to send him from the house, but as he continued to suffer I suggested that he consult a doctor. He did nothing. The day of his death he was under the influence of a strong drug that made him delirious. He insisted on coming to the table, and as I knew what he suspected I made a point of drinking only what he drank and of eating from the same plate. At the dessert he threw himself at my feet and begged my pardon for having suspected me. He said he knew now that he was being poisoned by 'that horrible Palmire'. And he begged me to aid him in fastening the guilt on her. As I tried naturally to defend her, he left me abruptly and locked himself in his room. You know the rest. It was I who asked for an autopsy." '

"Lieutenant Jacobini stopped.

" 'And that convinced you of her innocence?' I asked.

" 'No,' he answered. 'If Olympe expected something of the nature of Sabin's letter, I was ready for an explanation such as she gave me with a few tears thrown into the bargain. My next remark to my bride of an hour was very abrupt. "And what about the tali-tali, Olympe? What have you done with it?" I asked.

" 'She started and turned a deathly white. "Oh," she moaned, "so you think that I poisoned him with tali-tali?"*

" 'I took her by the wrist and it was like holding a hand of marble. "Listen, Olympe: Hubert died of an accident. I'll grant that and it doesn't matter to me; but Delphin was my friend and he and Dr Sabin died the same death. They were both poisoned by the tali-tali which leaves no trace. It was I who gave the poison to Delphin that he might analyse it and find an antidote if possible. I brought it back with me on my last return from Africa and I want to know what has become of it. It is a terrible poison which the wizards down there give to the unfortunates who are suspected of having brought the anger of bad spirits on the village. Its victims are legion . . . I am responsible for what it has done in France . . . What have you done with the tali-tali, Olympe?"

" 'Olympe looked up at me with frozen eyes. She was no longer crying. "There is no more tali-tali," she answered.

" ' "Since when?" I asked brutally, trying to gain control over her obstinate mind, which was clearly fighting against me now.

" ' "Since I asked Delphin to destroy it. That was a gift, sir, which you should never have made, not that I believe that he died of it, but because it would have been your fault if he had

* The tali-tali of which Lieutenant Jacobini speaks here is certainly a close relative of the poison described in André Demaison's work. In the *Diato* is written: "A man was hovering over the cauldron in which boiled the roots and bark of the sacred tree. At its name the children were terrified and the adults lost their mind: but the sorcerer, who was now pouring rice into the horrible soup, had declared that the poison could only harm those who sucked the marrow from the bones of their own kind. . . ." And this is the picture of those put to the test: "The unfortunates fell to the ground, letting out hoarse and horrible cries of pain. The bodies curled into a ball like partridges wounded by the hunter's bullet, or ducks with their necks cut before life is lost with the flow of blood." The tali-tali of which Lieutenant Jacobini speaks produces fulminating effects if taken in a large dose. In other cases the poisoning may be slow. Sometimes it takes twenty-four hours for it to manifest itself in all its force. The victim, as happened to Dr Sabin, seems to have fallen from an epileptic fit.

killed me with it. Was it the poison that was closed in the belly of a mahogany fetish covered with bizarre signs and curious designs burned into the wood?"

" ' "That was it, Olympe. There is no possible error. You know the tali-tali well."

" ' "Yes, Delphin used this poison and the barks of the tree which you brought him to make some experiments which interested me, much more than the rest of his work, as a matter of fact. His test-tubes and apparatus amused me in the beginning, but one tires of everything. I soon noticed, however, that Delphin was not well, and I blamed his languor on the bad air of the laboratory. I asked him to give up his work for a little while. He would not, so I asked him at least to do me the favour of destroying the tali-tali. He answered that there was nothing to fear because the tali-tali was only fatal to those who drank it and that he was certainly not crazy enough to drink the liquid, which he had already tried out on chickens and rabbits. He was amused at my childishness, but I gave him no peace until he had destroyed the tali-tali in front of me and Palmire. Tired of fighting with me about it he threw the fetish and the poison into the fire and it was burned up in a moment."

" ' "How did the poison act in the fire?"

" ' "First there was a long green flame like a sky rocket and that was followed by a suffocating vapour which we ran from. As for the fetish itself, it was nothing more than an ember which flashed a last grimace before falling into ashes. That is all, sir, and I have nothing else to tell you, but if it was to hear this that you married me you might as well have dispensed with the ceremony. I would have given you the information just the same, and perhaps I would have loved you afterwards. But now please leave this house and never let me see you again." '

"When Jacobini reached this point he stopped and rolled himself a cigarette.

" 'And then?' I asked.

" 'Then I left her to question Palmire. I forced her to tell of the tali-tali also. I attacked her from all sides. She's an ignorant peasant and she could not have invented the chemical effects which she had seen in the fire. All she said agreed to the letter with what Olympe had told me. I asked her all kinds of questions which Olympe could not have foreseen. I went on into other matters and at the end of my investigation I went back to Olympe and threw myself on my knees before her. She pardoned me, Zinzin, because besides being honest she is also very good.'

" 'Possibly,' I said, 'but she is not proud!'

"As you can well imagine, I did not go to call on them, but I saw Jacobini eight days later. An awful anguish was visible on his pale, restless face.

" 'Zinzin,' he said to me in a hoarse voice, 'I think I'm infected with it, too. But perhaps it is only an idea. Yes, an idea! Even the thought of that tali-tali is enough to drive one mad.'

"I didn't have time to say a word. He had already gone and I was never to see him alive again.

"And this is the frightful tragedy which occurred the next day according to the police, who with help from the dying Jacobini and Palmire's statements reconstructed the scene.

"At noon, Jacobini, who had not seen his wife since morning, went to the pavilion. He was filled with the darkest presentiments in spite of the fact that he tried to free himself of the idea of poison by trying to believe that his illness was due to swamp fevers which he had suffered from in the tropics.

"Luncheon was served there, and, as Jacobini entered, a door closed hurriedly at the end of the room. At the same time he heard furtive steps and the sound of a box being closed. He ran to the door, half opened it and saw Olympe engaged in low conversation with Palmire. She seemed very much troubled.

"At that moment a terrible cramp seized him in the intestines and he let the door close, having only strength enough to drop on the sofa. With one hand he had unconsciously taken hold of Olympe's work-box, which was badly closed and showed bits of fine linen. Jacobini's fingers, clutching at the lid feverishly from pain, opened it and fumbled in the lace. Suddenly they struck a hard object and he stood up, haggard and mad . . .

"In his hand he held the fetish of death, the horrible phial, the hideous tali-tali which Olympe and Palmire had sworn was destroyed, burned before them. Olympe had lied. Olympe had poisoned him as she had poisoned the other two. He was to suffer the atrocious death which had tortured his predecessors.

"Overcoming the agony for a few minutes, Jacobini poured what was left of the poison into a bottle of wine on the table. There was enough left for a terrible dose, and then he waited for his wife.

"She was not long in coming. She kissed him and asked him how he felt this morning. He replied that he felt much better, but that the fever had not completely left him and that he was thirsty.

" 'Then you must drink something, darling,' she said.

"He did not wait for her to pour the wine out and filled two glasses himself.

" 'But you know that the doctors have forbidden me wine,' she said, 'and that I only drink water.'

"He insisted that she drink with him in the same glass, as they had often done. She turned her head away. He seized her brutally, threw her head back and savagely pinched her nostrils, thus forcing her to drink. As she cried with fear, she spoke. 'Perhaps you would have preferred another glass,' he said, and showed her the tali-tali.

"She cried for help, but suddenly put her hand to her abdomen and was taken with a horrible cramp. At the same time the pain clutched at him, and they fell together on the sofa. They shrieked together, agonised together, clutched and scratched and bit each other. They pulled at each other like wild beasts. They twisted and writhed, contorting themselves in the same hell.

"Jacobini had still strength enough to insult her, naming the first victims. 'You won't kill any more. You are going to die. You are going to die with me.'

"But the pain was too great. It seemed as though there was hell within him. He pulled weapons down from the walls, and he tried to stab himself with a knife and so end the horror at one blow; but he only succeeded in making a terrible wound. Then he turned the steel towards Olympe and slit her open from top to bottom like an animal. The room echoed with her last howl.

"Possessed by a thousand demons he smashed her skull, pierced her like a pin-cushion, pulled out her eyes and cut her into pieces. She was nothing more than a bleeding, nameless horror when the servants rushed into the room.

"But Jacobini did not die until the next morning and in his few moments of lucidity narrated the hideous details of their abominable martyrdom. The assistant district attorney who at one time had hoped to marry her was present, and he returned home and went to bed ill. During the night he was so delirious that they thought he would lose his mind and so add one more victim to the list."

Zinzin stopped. Perspiration beaded his temples. He let out a sort of groan.

"The most horrible part," he went on, "is the fact that she had done nothing."

"Oh!" the others exclaimed.

"Yes, she was innocent. I learned that the other day, only the other day."

"Palmire had done it all!" Gaubert exclaimed.

"As to her," said Zinzin with a terrible laugh, "the police took her and kept her. You can well understand that I did everything in my power to have her given full punishment. All she did was to say no, and to cry about Olympe. Concerning her mistress, however, she gave us explanations which dumbfounded us. They were so utterly stupid or naive. For example, when they asked her: 'If your mistress was innocent, she would not have told her husband that the tali-tali had been destroyed before the two of you."

" 'Bah, that is simple,' Palmire answered. 'We agreed between us to say that it had been because there were already rumours about and we did not want to be suspected; besides we did not know what had become of the tali-tali because we really believed that Monsieur Delphin had burned it all the day that he threw a few drops in to please Madame.'

"Yes, she said just that," Zinzin went on, "and she was hissed and hooted. I cried louder than the rest."

"And what was she sentenced to?" asked Chaulieu.

"Death," replied Zinzin in a whisper.

"But they don't execute women?"

"No . . . Her sentence was changed to life imprisonment. She died in her cell about ten years ago. I learned that the other day also."

"And did she repent? Did she confess?" Michel asked.

"No," Zinzin answered, looking at us like a madman, "and she had nothing to confess . . . *She, too, was innocent!*"

"Good God!" Chaulieu exclaimed.

"But then, who was guilty?" Gaubert asked.

"A man who has just died and confessed on his deathbed. After the tragedy he left the town and settled not far from here. Yes, he died the other day at Mourillon. That man had owned some property which touched the edge of Olympe's estate in the far corner where the pavilion was."

"But who was the man? – one of the twelve?"

"Yes, one of the twelve – the twelfth, to be exact! He naturally could not ever hope to marry Olympe, because of course she would never go through with eleven husbands after such deaths, but he eliminated those who had been happier than he . . . and at the end he had fixed it so that the evidence all pointed to Olympe.

"Do you remember, when the twelfth suitor arrived that day when we were all lined up in the drawing-room – the arrival of Monsieur Pacifire, the registrar – what fun Olympe made of him and how we had all laughed when she placed him at the foot of the line? Yes, we made fun of Monsieur Pacifire when he came into the room! Well, he avenged himself, that man!"

THE INN OF TERROR

"SPEAKING OF WOMEN," said Chaulieu, "I would never wish any of you a honeymoon like the one I took with my first wife. Besides coming very close to losing our lives . . . But here's the story without any further preamble. On my return from Saigon, I asked headquarters for a furlough and took advantage of it to marry little Maria-Luce of Mourillon, as had been previously decided. Her father had died in Madagascar and she lived with her grandfather.

"We went to Switzerland on our honeymoon. It was my idea, because at heart I'm a staid fellow, a landlubber, and I hate adventures. If I was a sea captain for twenty years, it was simply to follow the family tradition and to please my parents, but the very thought of it in the beginning made me seasick.

"Well, there we were in Switzerland, my young bride and I, as in the days of Töppfer. We were very much in love, and . . . Have you ever been in Soleure?"

"I was married in Borneo," chuckled Dorat, the biggest wag in the party of old sea-dogs who spun their yarns on the terrace of the Café of the Old Wet-Dock in Toulon.

"I see . . . Well, Soleure might be called the capital of French Switzerland – a long, quiet street with picture sign-boards swinging on their rods at the slightest puff of wind from the Wesseinstein.

"The Wesseinstein is one of the summits in the Jura mountains. It rises at the north-west of the town. More than one tourist has lost his way in the gorges and paths of the forest, and there are no hotels before reaching the summit, with the exception of one which at the time boasted a very sinister reputation.

"Two years before our trip, the town board had discovered, at the bottom of a well and in a nearby grotto, twelve skeletons and some objects belonging to travellers who had found a fatal hospitality there.

"The inquest investigations brought to light the fact that the crimes had been committed by a couple who had so thoroughly terrorised the neighbourhood that even the death of the two innkeepers, the dreadful Weisbachs – you may remember the story perhaps; it was in all the newspapers at the time – did not loosen any tongues. You see, a few old-timers in the mountains had suspected some of the goings-on; but Jean Weisbach had made it very clear that he did not care to have people meddling in his business, and they had let bad enough alone.

"The innkeepers had died quietly in their beds, in the end, rich and esteemed, as also did their factotum, one Daniel. When the mare's nest was discovered, the examining magistrates were able after questioning hither and yon and forcing some stubborn old neighbours to speak, to reconstruct the crimes. The most important witness was an old woman with a goitre, who related certain horrible details which showed that, besides a grim greed for money, the Weisbachs had had a strain of sadism and cruelty in them that has rarely been exceeded.

"Naturally, this story was the chief topic of conversation in Soleure. The travellers, who were to go by coach to the peak of the Wesseinstein, to sleep in the hotel made famous by Napoleon, and from there go back into France through the Belfort gap, promised themselves by all means to stop for a drink, half way up, at the 'Inn of Blood'. It had been called that as much because of the story as for the colour it was painted. To stop there was one of the things planned in the trip up the mountain. While the driver gave the horses a drink, the tourists went inside to the bar and gossiped with the new proprietors. These two had been there only a year. Their predecessors, the immediate successors of the Weisbachs, had left the premises, as soon as the scandal broke, on the grounds that they were ruined. But the Scheffers, being shrewder, had said to themselves that there were plenty of fools in the world, whose curiosity would probably make them rich. Their reasoning had not been bad, if one could believe what was said in town. All the strangers now passing through Soleure wanted, of all things, to see the 'Inn of Blood', and some even went so far as to sleep there.

"The weather was fine the day that Maria-Luce and I left for the Wesseinstein by diligence. We had had an excellent lunch and were prepared to enjoy a lovely drive, and live a few ideally romantic hours like a chapter from a novel. We had left our luggage in Soleure and were to return there for it. Maria-Luce had only a small handbag with her. Ah! we narrowly missed never returning to Soleure and also lived that romantic chapter of ours in a way we would never have wished! You will see why . . .

"When I think of it! . . . Perhaps that is what killed my good little Maria-Luce! . . . She was so pretty, so gay, so full of life . . . with such a clear lovely skin, and cheeks like roses. Well, such is life – a never-tiring destroyer . . . I often wonder why we are born at all . . .

"Ah! we were in love! . . . I had hired the coupé of the stage-coach just for the two of us, so that we could be by ourselves and kiss when we felt like it, which was only natural after all!

"Just as we were about to leave, a man and woman arrived on the scene . . . a handsome pair! I'll never forget them as long as I live, and with reason. They were Italians: he, a big, handsome man, too handsome, in the thirties, with big, dark eyes like velvet, the kind of eyes they have in Italy and that make the signorinas lose their heads . . . flashing teeth, olive skin, clean-shaven and the appearance of an actor. He was one, in fact, a tenor who was already well-known and had had a brilliant success at La Scala in Milan . . . Antonio Ferretti as we learned later . . . Amiable, jovial, in perfect health, he felt that he owned the world.

"His companion, who adored him openly with every look, was obviously his, body and soul. She was a young, ravishingly beautiful woman, as golden-haired as a Venetian, which she was, and belonging to the highest aristocracy. Her name belonged to history from that day on, judicial history, alas! . . . Countess Olivia Orsino. The handsome tenor had abducted her.

"I'm telling you all this at the start to get rid of it, so that you can understand the people at first sight, which was more than we did; all we considered at the moment was the fact that an annoying couple wanted to join us in the coupé, under the pretence that the interior compartment of the coach was already practically full, and would even have driven us out if it had been possible. An argument ensued, of course; the handsome tenor's free and easy manner irritated me, and I was even more annoyed because I had been so pleased with the idea of just the two of us taking this little trip together. If he had been more polite, however, Antonio Ferretti would certainly have won his cause, because after all I'm not a roughneck, and as I said before, his companion was charming.

"Maria-Luce advised me to give in, but one word spoiled everything, something like 'damned savages, these French'. I slammed the door violently, and as I had already paid for the four seats I insisted on my right and they were obliged to sit with the others. As a matter of fact, if it annoyed them to travel by diligence they had only to rent a carriage, but it wasn't an easy thing in those days before automobiles to find horses and carriage to go up to the Wesseinstein. They had to be wagons specially built like the diligence, with a hanging rod always ready to grip the road in case of slipping back, which was always to be feared. If I have lingered over this incident it is because it assumed a terrible importance, alas! for some of us.

"Our drive started through a pretty little cut in the hills, fresh, wooded, resounding with rippling waters, and in which nestles a little retreat, famous in that neighbourhood – it was that of Saint Verène, Verena Einsiedolei, if I'm not mistaken – with chapels, grottos, overhanging rocks, and from time to time, beautiful blocks of Soleure marble which caught the sun and shone in great, blinding spots.

"Three hours later we were in the depths of the forest, far from any dwelling, and the sun had disappeared. Big clouds floated between us and the mountain peaks, and before long a black veil hid the entire valley. At the same time a dull noise like thunder rumbled down towards us; but it was not the thunder yet: it was a heavy sledge, loaded with wood, which tumbled down the road on its runners with overwhelming rapidity. A young boy, perched up on top, steered it.

"It was under the threat of a coming storm that we finally caught sight of the 'Inn of Blood'. In the livid light of the twilight, it was not a pleasant sight with its squat, thick walls, barred windows and the old, arched door, studded with iron, which led to the famous well. The whole was covered with a horrible, brownish paint which, it seems, is used on the arms of the guillotine.

" 'Heavens, but it's ugly!' Maria-Luce cried, and it really must have been, for that afternoon, I can assure you, we were both in a mood to find everything lovely. We had not been bored with each other on the ride up! We had told each other stories, we had made plans for the future, and we had kissed to the health of our two Italians.

"Just as the diligence stopped in front of this sinister dwelling, a regular torrent of rain, accompanied by flashes of lightning and great growls of thunder, came down. We rushed into the inn, or rather into an enormous kitchen at the end of which was a tremendous fireplace large enough to burn a tree. At the present moment, however, only an honest little fire of dried branches was crackling away, and above it in an honest little pot, hung from a pot-hook, boiled a beef stew which smelled excellent. Before us stood the innkeeper, round-bellied like a barrel, with a pleasant manner, small, twinkling eyes peering out from creases of fat, and three chins, the tamest ogre in the world, all smiles.

" 'Are you reassured?' I asked Maria-Luce.

" 'Yes,' she answered, 'he won't have us cooked in that little pot, and he seems delighted! . . . But what weather!'

"As a matter of fact, the driver had unharnessed the horses and got them under shelter because he was beginning to worry about the equilibrium of the carriage under the repeated claps of thunder. I asked him how long we would be staying here.

" 'An hour,' he answered. 'I'll be off again in an hour, no matter what the weather does!'

"I figured that we would arrive at the hotel at the Wesseinstein in the middle of the night, if we arrived at all, because the road skirted a precipice on the right. I came to a rapid decision, and Maria-Luce agreed with me; so, taking the innkeeper aside, I asked him if he had a room.

" 'I have two,' the stout fellow answered, looking at me with a bantering twinkle in his eyes. 'You want to sleep here?'

" 'Yes. Show me your rooms!'

" 'If you'll just wait a moment until I have served the lady and gentleman in the drawing-room, I'll be at your service.'

"What he called the drawing-room was a small room off the kitchen, furnished with a round table covered with oil-cloth, four chairs, and a few prints of the battles of the First Empire hanging on the walls, which were whitewashed. Our two Italians had made for this luxurious and comfortable nook on leaving the coach, in order to escape from associations from which they had already suffered.

"When Scheffer, the innkeeper, opened the door which they had closed, I saw the handsome tenor at the window looking out at the landscape sadly. His companion was seated with her elbows on the table and did not seem any more cheerful.

"The innkeeper came back to us.

" 'There are two more who want to sleep here! A drive in this rain doesn't attract them. You had better hurry about choosing your room, because, between you and me, there is only one decent one!'

"You can well imagine that I lost no time. We went up a stairway as steep as a ladder, that led on the left to the attic, which was directly over the kitchen, and on the right to a corridor which went to what was called 'the travellers' room'. This room was famous: it was here that almost all the murdered guests had slept.

" 'You aren't afraid,' Scheffer chuckled, on opening the door; 'but then, of course, nowadays only honeymooners come here.'

" 'That is true of us.'

" 'Oh, then I won't worry about you,' he replied; 'you won't have any bad dreams! Have you any luggage?'

" 'No, we left it at Soleure.'

"It seemed to me that this detail irritated him. That may have been an idea that I invented later. Later, I also remembered that he eyed Maria-Luce's bag, the jewels she wore, and even the big ring I wore, very keenly. But I won't swear to it. He did it very quickly before leaving us. Outside it was still pouring, but the thunder had stopped.

"In the fading light of the day, this room seemed a very peaceful retreat to us. It was large and clean, with light, flowered wallpaper; a big bed with white sheets, and an enormous red eiderdown quilt, a comfortable Morris chair, the mantel decorated with bouquets of orange blossoms, under a glass globe, and two pictures taken from Monsieur de Chateaubriand's *Atala and the Last of the Abencérages*, the subject of which I explained to Maria-Luce.

" 'We'll be very comfortable here,' she remarked, 'and if you were nice you'd have a fire built on the hearth and we'd dine together in our room!'

" 'Good idea. I'll go right down and tell our landlord.'

" 'I'll come with you!' she cried. 'You're not going to leave me alone in this room!'

" 'Ah! it bothers you just the same. . . .'

" 'Heavens, yes, when I think——'

" 'Very well, come along, and don't think!'

"We were at the head of the stairs in front of the door of the attic when we heard the Italian's voice.

" 'But this isn't a room!' Antonio was exclaiming. 'It's a garret! It's a dirty hole! . . .'

" 'It's the only thing I have to give you,' the innkeeper answered. 'I have already explained that my other room is taken!'

"The door opened and we found ourselves face to face with the two Italians and the innkeeper.

" 'Ah, you again, signor!' the tenor exclaimed. 'You must admit that we are out of luck.'

"I could not stop a smile. I had caught sight of an iron bed in one corner of the attic which was stuffed with all the dull, rusty articles that one is accustomed to store in such places.

" 'In fact,' I answered, 'this is not a very comfortable place to sleep in, especially when one is accustomed to a certain amount of luxury. Do you know what I would do in your place? Now that the coupé is free, I would leave with the diligence!'

" 'He is right,' agreed the signora.

" 'He is making fun of us!' the other muttered between his teeth.

"I saw that there might be trouble, so I carried Maria-Luce off and went back down into the large, public room of the inn.

"In spite of the rain, the other travellers had wanted to see the well where the executioners had thrown their victims, and they all returned dripping wet. They ordered hot grogs while the innkeeper, still joking a bit sarcastically, gave details:

" 'They probably didn't drink the water from that well – everyone has his little niceties – but the peasants around here did. After all it didn't matter much, because the Weisbachs did things neatly. They cleaned their skeletons well. They boiled for hours and hours in a cauldron that hung from that very pot-hook!'

"Upon which, the travellers asked to see the cauldron, the pitchfork, the axe, and the knife, all the instruments of torture, in fact, that had become famous in this horrible affair.

" 'They are in the little dungeon . . . and my wife has the key.'

"Madame Scheffer, detained at some forester's because of the weather, took her time about returning. The driver announced in the meantime that he was ready to leave, and the room emptied itself in a moment.

"The Italians did not come down until after the diligence had left. They seemed to have made up their minds to make the best of their part in the adventure and ordered dinner. We watched them out of the corner of our eyes, and Maria-Luce was very much amused. I was extremely polite and opened the conversation.

" 'If I had been alone, I would have given my room up willingly . . .'

" 'A bad night is soon over,' the Italian answered me with a smile.

"The woman, whom I'll call Countess Orsino although I did not know her name at the time, was charming to Maria-Luce.

" 'We have been cheated,' she said to her; 'this inn is not at all horrible.'

"A door at the end of the room opened, and Madame Scheffer, the innkeeper's wife, entered. She rid herself of an enormous coat and hood, and as she did so we could not control the chill of terror that ran up our spines. The sight was worse than horrible: it was sinister. Her hideousness was due mostly to her squinting eyes and enormous, grinning mouth. Aside from that, she had sparkling teeth, beautiful golden hair, and a nose that was a bit thick, with ferociously sensual nostrils. I don't know what Madame Weisbach was like, but this woman certainly seemed to exhale an odour of blood. She was strong and still young, about thirty-eight, with firm limbs, and hands used to men's work.

"Behind her came the manservant, whom we had not yet seen. He was thick-set, slightly humpbacked, and he limped. A redhead with the face of a brute.

"He threw down the burden he was hidden under on the paving and gave a sigh of relief. Then he looked at us in silence and lifted a trapdoor under the stairs. He lighted a lamp, which was there prepared, and disappeared down into the cellar, dragging his bundle behind him. The innkeeper was cleaning the dirty wineglasses and no one had said a word. The three of them had looked at us in silence, that was all.

" 'I'm frightened this time,' Maria-Luce whispered to me.

" 'Yes, it's beginning to become more interesting,' I answered, 'but don't get worked up and we'll have some fun out of it.'

"The innkeeper was the first to break the silence after his wife had disappeared into the cellar behind the servant.

" 'What do you think of my wife?' he asked. 'She fits in well in an inn like this, doesn't she? I couldn't have chosen better! . . .'

"I joined in the game. 'Yes, it's quite a good trick.'

"The little countess had retreated into the shadow of her handsome tenor, and he remarked pleasantly: 'Madame Scheffer would be very good-looking if she didn't squint.'

" 'If she hadn't squinted, I would not have married her,' the innkeeper answered. 'Weisbach's wife squinted! And I wonder if you noticed my manservant . . . he's humpbacked and bow-legged like Daniel, the Weisbachs' servant. I had to go all the way to Chaux-de-Fonds to find him.'

" 'Why don't you laugh, Olivia?' asked the tenor, who seemed to be enjoying himself.

" 'Did they ever murder anyone in the attic?' Olivia gasped.

" 'Did they ever murder anyone in the attic!' Scheffer exclaimed. 'Well, I should say so! I have all the newspapers if you want to look them over. Daniel slept in the attic and stood guard over the travellers in the other room. When he believed that they were safely asleep, he would knock three times on the floor, and the Weisbachs, who kept themselves in readiness for the signal, came up . . .

" 'Sometimes the deed was easily and quietly done; other times there was a scuffle. The woman with the goitre told how Mengal from Breslau, president of the court of justice, defended himself so well that his wife was able to escape. But on leaving the room, the unfortunate woman rushed into the attic where Daniel always waited, holding himself in readiness to help. He broke her skull in with one blow of the axe . . . You will see the axe! . . .'

" 'How horrible!' moaned the countess.

" 'Oh, that's nothing,' the innkeeper went on, shrugging his shoulders; 'there are lots of other tales about them that are more interesting than this. And I'm not making them up. There's the one about the beautiful brunette chained down in the grotto. But you ought to reconstruct the scene of the tale for yourselves in the little dungeon, if you are fond of such things! You will also see the pitchfork that the Weisbachs used to caress the little brunette! . . .'

"I felt Maria-Luce's hand tremble in mine.

" 'Give me a light,' I said to the innkeeper and when I had lighted my pipe: 'Scheffer, you're a dirty fraud!'

" 'By Gad, no! What about the inquest? . . . and the newspapers?'

" 'Possible. . . . But you make me laugh with your axe and your pitchfork! It's as though you told me that the Weisbachs cooked their victims in that pot over there!'

" 'You're a shrewd one,' he burst out with a roar of laughter. 'But I found the cauldron I need yesterday. My wife went to pay for it today and the man brought it back with some other little things that won't go badly with the landscape! Yes, it's true, I'm helping the atmosphere along a little . . . It was my idea . . . And when everything is just as it was *before*, people will feel that they are back in the times of the Weisbachs . . . But you must believe! . . . When I tell you that this is the cauldron, this the axe, and this the pitchfork, you must believe, or there's no fun in it . . . but then you're not an amateur in such things! . . . What I am doing is for the amateurs who specialise in horrors! The fact that it is the actual dungeon, the well, and the inn, is a good start and with a little imagination it won't be hard to believe that the crimes have just been committed . . . without counting the fact that my wife and servant are a stroke of genius! . . . I hope to be rich in ten years. When I think that the people who were here before me had the travellers' room done over and added a drawing-room! . . . The fools! As though it were possible to ruin the "Inn of Blood" like that!'

"He sighed and went on, 'You see, I'm not trying to put anything over on you. You're not out for thrills, so I have shown you the inside of everything. But there are people who would be angry with me if I were to give the show away. There are some, you know, who *love it!* . . . Don't be afraid, little lady,' he said to the Countess, 'if the idea that you are going to sleep in the attic where they murdered that poor woman upsets you, I'll have a mattress put in the drawing-room.'

" 'No, we'll sleep in the attic,' Antonio Ferretti declared.

" 'Very well. And you,' the innkeeper asked, turning to me, 'does the idea of sleeping in the "travellers' room" bother you?'

" 'Not a bit, not a bit! Does it, Maria-Luce?'

" 'Oh, the whole place frightens me,' Maria-Luce answered.

"At that, we three men burst out laughing and the women joined us at the end, but only half-heartedly.

"Madame Scheffer reappeared out of the trapdoor, followed by the servant, and we stopped laughing immediately. Only Scheffer seemed vastly amused by the effect that his wife had had on us. He called out to his servant: 'Daniel!' . . . *like the other one!*

"He ordered him to wring the neck of two chickens, but Olivia said that she was not hungry and that a cup of bouillon would satisfy her.

" 'Excuse me, but I am,' Antonio protested, 'and a chicken won't frighten me!'

" 'And you?' I asked Maria-Luce.

" 'Nor me,' she answered, squeezing up close to me; 'that is the only thing in the house that doesn't frighten me.'

" 'Shall we dine together?' Antonio asked. He had obviously forgotten the incident of the diligence.

" 'No, thank you,' I answered; 'I've had a fire lit in our room and my wife and I will dine alone in our quarters.'

" 'It's very nice up there,' he replied, smiling. 'I have seen the room. You're in luck. I can understand how people sleep there *even at the risk of being murdered*!'

" 'You are cheerful!'

" 'Oh, I'm only speaking of those who were before you.'

"The innkeeper started to rattle some keys. He had just lighted the lamps, as night had completely fallen.

" 'While waiting for dinner, I'll show you around. The rain has stopped and we can go to the well, to the grotto, and in the stable.'

"The women hesitated, but we persuaded them to follow us. The innkeeper went ahead with a swinging lantern; and in the stable, in front of the well, and in the grotto, which was about a hundred yards from the inn and the existence of which had been ignored for a long time, he reconstructed the whole story – and

more. He put in a few details of his own! The crimes of the
Peyrebelle Inn were mere trifles compared to the crimes of the
'Inn of Blood'!

"The Weisbachs had made a sort of crematory oven out of one
end of the grotto, and some fragments of human bones, too large
to be confused with the bones of sheep, had been found there.

"It was useless trying to be strong-minded; we all came back
from that little expedition somewhat upset. We were glad to
re-enter the big room of the inn with its cheerful hearth . . . and
yet! . . . Yes, but over the fire, two chickens were turning on the
spit and filled the air with an extremely pleasant aroma. The
bow-legged servant basted them from time to time with their
juice, meanwhile polishing up a big leather basin.

" 'What are you doing?' I asked him.

"He lifted his brute face up towards me and went on with his
rubbing.

" 'Don't ask Daniel questions,' the innkeeper said with a little
laugh. 'It's a waste of time, because he won't answer you. Not
that he is dumb, but I have ordered him to be mute like the other,
who really was! You understand?'

" 'Oh, yes, I understand. Congratulations, you haven't overlooked a thing.'

" 'Nothing. And when the cauldron is on the hearth, you'll see
what a sensation I'll make when I repeat the story told to the
judge by the woman with the goitre.'

" 'What was that?' Antonio asked.

" 'Why, the story of what happened to her when she first
awoke to the fact that she was working for very peculiar people.
One night when she came in from her washing, she found a
roaring fire on the hearth. She went closer to see what they were
cooking in the pot, and she lifted the cover; but Weisbach appeared on the run and gave her a blow that sent her reeling
against the wall. But she had seen! . . . She had seen a man's
head turning around in the bouillon, surrounded by chunks
of flesh.

" ' "You see," Weisbach said to her, "curiosity is always
punished. If I did what was right, I'd send you to the bottom of

the pot to find out what is going on there! But I need you. In the meantime, keep your mouth shut!"

" 'The wretched woman threw herself at his feet, swearing that she would never speak. And she stayed with him, because she knew that they would never let her go alive! From that day on, they talked openly before her, and there were even some nights when they forced her to help them in many ways. They would tell her to follow them down to the grotto and close the argument by kicking her down ahead of them . . .

" 'Come, let's go down there now. It's the best part of the whole place.'

"And he picked up his lantern again.

"The women exchanged looks; then, catching sight of the bow-legged man who was staring at them covertly while he continued to polish his cauldron, they made up their minds and we went down into the cellar behind Scheffer. A slimy stairway, a greasy cord, weird shadows thrown by his flickering light . . . it was awful! We soon heard ringing blows like those of a hammer beating against chains. And, as a matter of fact, that is what it was. At the end of a subterranean passage the man threw open a door and we saw another lantern on the damp earth of the vault. Madame Scheffer was crouched on the ground, busy fastening a piece of chain to a ring in the cave wall, from which hung a lantern. At the end of the chain there was an iron collar. She had her back to us and did not bother even to look up, but continued her hammering with the violence of a madwoman. At last she stopped a moment.

" 'That,' the man explained, 'I have had to have done. But it's old iron just the same. The marks of the hammer won't show as soon as it has rusted, and some people will be even able to find blood-stains.'

" 'What a beast!' I murmured; 'there is no possible way of being bored with you!'

" 'No, eh? Nor with my wife! . . . Wait, and she'll give you a thrill. She'll tell you the story of the pretty little brunette who was imprisoned in this cave. It's worth the trouble of listening . . .'

" 'You ought to set up your little trick in Paris, Boulevard

Rochechouart, near the Café of the Yellow-Hammer. You'd be a big success.'

" 'I know,' he answered. 'I've travelled. There are plenty of fools in the world.'

"The grotto was not very big. Nevertheless, there was room enough for a little exhibit. An enormous rusty knife, a saw, an axe and all the necessary implements for an innkeeper who conducts his business in the way that the deceased Weisbach did, hung from nails embedded between the cracks of the stones. In one place were a pitchfork and an ox-goad; against the wall were some tongs. Some shapeless, colourless rags also hung from stalactites. Once, it seems, they had been clothes, and in another spot was a pile of debris which included some pieces of old leather, all that remained of some shoes.

" 'Read my collection of newspapers and you will see that all this stuff is mentioned. I haven't made up a thing. Unfortunately, the police kept all the originals and I had to replace them as best I could!' He laughed and said to his wife, 'Go to it; it's your turn now.'

"She stood up and came towards us and we shrank back. I shall see those squinting eyes and that big mouth all the rest of my life. And what a setting! The whole was brought into fantastic relief by the fierce, blood-red light thrown by the two lanterns, one of which was still on the ground. It was like a horrible, evil etching . . .

"The woman put out her arms and grasped the pitchfork almost greedily, and as she spoke she glared at the little countess with such ferocity that the other was forced to turn away . . . And what a voice! It was like a sound from hell.

" 'And yet you know,' Scheffer said to us, 'she only drinks her little swallow of brandy in the morning after her coffee like the rest of the world. Good old Annette!' (*He called her Annette, like the other one!*). 'You will see what a wonder she is.'

" 'Perhaps one of the ladies would like to try the iron collar,' she began. 'It doesn't matter that Madame is blonde: it would be just as effective.'

"But the suggestion was not very well received, and Annette smiled a horrible smile!

" 'Everyone to his own taste. This is what happened, according to the woman with the goitre. A beautiful brunette arrived one afternoon accompanied by a middle-aged gentleman. They were obviously rich and had lots of jewellery. A mishap to their carriage forced them to take shelter at the inn for the night, and the coachman, who went back to Soleure, was to return the next day with another carriage for them. When he arrived the next morning, he was informed that the two had departed early in the morning and that they had left money for him. He took the amount coming to him and went off without bothering any further about his customers. But his customers had never left the inn . . .

" 'The gentleman, knocked unconscious by Daniel and cut up into pieces by Weisbach, was already in the cauldron. As to the lovely brunette, she was still alive in the little grotto . . . She lived there for fifteen days, according to the woman with the goitre. Every night as soon as the inn was closed they went down to see her. They had her chained down there to this iron collar. One evening the woman with the goitre heard cries and slipped down into the cellar, but Weisbach, who had sharp ears, discovered her. He dragged her into the vault. "You want to see?" he said to her. "Then see you must . . . see what will happen to you if you talk." And she saw . . .

" 'The lovely brunette was there, completely naked and chained as I have already described. She was just one piece of torn flesh, and Weisbach's wife, now with the pitchfork, now with the goad, was stroking her ribs.'

"So saying, Madame Scheffer went into action. And what she was telling was less horrible than what she did! Half bent over herself, with a savage light in her eyes, and that enormous mouth foaming at the corners, she hurled first her fork and then her goad where the chain hung. And she did it with a fire that suddenly ceased to be play and became a kind of madness and wild enjoyment.

" 'The slut!' she screamed, and the sound of her voice sent a chill up my spine; 'she killed the poor little brunette! like this! like this! and again! and again! She crushed in her ribs, tore the flesh, while the walls resounded with the other's cries of pain. "Now you're beautiful! Let your lover come now! Ah, and this, too. Now you are more beautiful than I!"

" 'I must tell you,' Madame Scheffer said, panting and turning towards us, or rather towards the little countess, who had to lean against the wall to keep from falling, 'I must explain that Weisbach's wife was as ugly as sin, and she squinted! Naturally, she could not bear the sight of beautiful eyes' – so saying Madame Scheffer stared straight into the little countess' eyes – 'without wanting to scratch them out!'

" 'Let's go! let's go!' Olivia Orsino cried; 'I won't stay here another second!' And she rushed from the vault.

"We all followed her, and Scheffer, who was behind, said with a great laugh, 'I told you she was priceless! She has learned her lesson well. But don't let it upset you. Aside from that, she is as gentle as a lamb . . . and an excellent cook, too, as you will see.'

"And then the woman herself, who had joined us, said, 'So I frightened you? Well, I must tell the story; it will make people come!'

"I felt Maria-Luce tremble and we were all a little pale when we came back into the big room. We looked at each other and finally burst out laughing . . . all except the countess.

" 'What a horrible, horrible woman!' she murmured.

" 'And with all that, you don't know the end of the story,' said Scheffer, jabbing at the chickens with a fork to see how nearly done they were. He stopped the string which turned the spit. 'They are done to a turn, and with a good salad . . . you'll praise our cook . . . The end of the story is this: The day when the woman with the goitre was dragged into the vault was the day in which Madame Weisbach scratched the little brunette's eyes out with the pitchfork. She would teach the other to have more beautiful eyes than her own!'

" ' "Squint now, squint now!" is what she shrieked,' Madame

Scheffer completed, loading herself with a pile of dishes from a large chest.

" 'Enough,' I said firmly, 'we've had enough of an appetiser; let's eat!'

" 'Do you know what the Italian woman said to me?' Maria-Luce whispered. 'She doesn't want us to leave them. Let's eat down here.'

" 'Oh no!' I protested; 'I'm sick of these stories and I want you all to myself.'

"We took leave of the other two and I led my wife upstairs. We had a little trouble in finding our room in that strange hallway. The stairs were so steep that we came near to toppling down them, and it made me think of the Weisbachs. The traveller would go up the stairs while the servant waited for him in the dark at the top and pushed him down to the innkeepers, who were waiting at the bottom. And that was the end of him.

"We, however, were a bit luckier, and, as there was only one room in the inn, we finally found it. But before locating it I opened doors into several other rooms filled with packing-cases and all sorts of débris. I wondered why, in an inn, they did not make use of so much precious space, and while Scheffer was serving us our supper, in front of a good fire and under a tame enough lamp, I could not help asking him for an explanation of this. He answered that it would be a great expense, useless perhaps . . . and finally after hesitating a moment he added:

" 'Besides it seems to me that the Weisbachs *did not care to have too many travellers at one time*!'

"And he left, after putting a bottle of champagne on the table and wishing us good-night.

" 'Did you hear?' Maria-Luce whispered to me as soon as he was gone; 'but why does he want to leave things in the same condition?'

" 'He hasn't been here long. Give him a chance. You're not going to begin imagining things, are you?'

"By the time supper was over, I had cheered her up again. We had emptied our bottle of champagne gaily and forgotten all about the horrors. We were just about to go to bed when a light knock came at the door . . . There was no bolt in this door, but there was a key and a sort of hook that fastened to a ring in the casing.

" 'Who is there?' I asked.

" 'Don't open!' Maria-Luce whispered. She was already terror-stricken, for we had made quite an evening of it and might well be supposed asleep . . .

" 'Open, open quickly,' came a heavy voice which I recognised as the Italian's.

"At that I opened the door and the man threw himself into the room, shutting the door behind him. He was very pale and seemed in the throes of the wildest emotion . . .

" 'I've come to warn you,' he exclaimed, his voice trembling with emotion. 'First of all, we can hear everything they say in the kitchen. These people are murderers. I heard his wife say to Scheffer: "We have nothing to fear. If they find the bones, *they'll think they belonged to that other affair!*" We're not going to stay another second in this den. I've found a rope in the attic and I've fastened it to the window-ledge that overlooks the outside of the house, not the courtyard. Get dressed and follow us!'

"Maria-Luce was already half undressed and I had thrown my coat on the chair.

" 'This is a fine tale!' I exclaimed, dumbfounded.

" 'You didn't see that woman's eyes,' said Maria-Luce, her teeth chattering with fright.

"Seeing that I was undecided, the Italian lost no time and left us. Maria-Luce was dressing hastily, shaking in every limb.

" 'Let's go! let's go!' she begged. 'You haven't even a revolver.'

"That was true. And besides it was impossible to oppose Maria-Luce. I took the bag, and two minutes later we were in the attic, after removing our shoes to make no noise. The little wooden door of the garret window was open and the cord fastened to the screw of a pulley. The Italians had already gone. We put our shoes on hastily, and it was then that I discovered a little streak of light coming through a crack in the floor. It came up from the kitchen, and I tried to peer through it. I saw nothing, but I could hear Scheffer's voice say: 'Which one shall we begin on?' "

Chaulieu had reached this point in his narrative, when Captain Michel hit the table with such a blow of his fist that the saucers under their glasses jumped.

"I expected that! What an original story! But in Paul-Louis Courier's tale the innkeeper says, 'Shall we kill them both?' and he was only referring to two chickens! You take us for geese, Chaulieu!"

"Wait a minute," said Chaulieu. "I don't know what this Paul-Louis thing of yours is – I don't know him from the man in the moon – and if you are geese, inform your respective relations of the fact . . . I'm telling the adventure just as it happened to me."

"Let him finish," said Dorat; "I'll bet he had forgotten all about love when he heard those words."

"Yes, old man, I certainly had, and so had Maria-Luce. And I can tell you we lost no time in making our escape! I made another knot in the cord and grasped hold of it. Maria-Luce, to whom I had given the bag, which contained quite a large sum of money and our toilet articles, got up on my shoulders, and when we reached the ground we ran for ten minutes without stopping. We started down towards Soleure by the first path we came to because we did not dare risk the main road. I expected to catch up to the Italians, but we lost ourselves in the pitch-black darkness. Slipping and sliding and falling on the soaked ground, we plunged on madly."

"You were frightened to death by that time," laughed Michel.

"I should say we were. I couldn't even stop Maria-Luce, who thought we were being pursued by bandits ready to shoot us down at any minute. The worst was that it began to rain again – and how! . . . Good Lord, what a night! . . . lost in a forest, torn and scratched by branches, and pelted with the heaviest kind of rain! Never in my life have I ever spent such hours. And I finally had to carry Maria-Luce, who was nothing more than a dripping bundle of rags . . . At last, a light! A peasant's cottage . . . They took us in, warmed us, and gave us a bed. They dried our clothes for us, and in emptying my pockets I found a piece of paper with a few words written on it in pencil:

"Thanks for the room. I leave you the coupé."

"I would have sworn it!" exclaimed Captain Michel. "You must be a fool."

"Wait a minute," Chaulieu said again. "I haven't finished! You can well imagine what a temper I was in over this stupid joke, which, considering Maria-Luce's condition, narrowly escaped being criminal . . . It was no use rubbing her; she stayed as cold as ice. During the night she was taken with a high fever and I sent to Soleure for a doctor. It was two days before we were able to leave those kind peasants.

"I had had enough of Switzerland, and we returned to Mourillon the shortest way possible; but alas! the good southern sun was not enough to cure Maria-Luce. She had always told me that her lungs were not very strong, and from that day on she began to cough. And when at last, a few years later, she stopped coughing she was dead."

Dorat coughed at that to show that he was still very much alive.

"Listen, poor old Chaulieu," he said, "we're all sorry, but as far as Maria-Luce's death is concerned, it is a misfortune which might have occurred under entirely different circumstances, after a damp walk in the woods, for example. The truth of the matter, as far as your story goes, is that they played a rotten joke on you, that's all."

"No!" Chaulieu growled; "not at all . . . *The story only begins to be interesting from now on!*

"The following year the Italian papers, and finally newspapers all over the world, were full of the disappearance of a man and a woman. And that is how we knew that our two Italians had been Antonio Ferretti and Countess Olivia Orsino. If we had had any doubts, which was impossible because the resemblance between them both was perfect, we would have been convinced by this fact: that they had been traced as far as Soleure, and there the trail ended!

"When Maria-Luce and I learned of this we looked at each other in silence, and the same terrible thought struck us both. The unfortunate pair had wanted to make fun of us. They had hidden in a corner of the hall and after our departure had slipped into our room, where the Scheffers had murdered them *in our place*!

"Well, what do you say to that?" he asked, enjoying the astonishment of his friends. "Not so bad, eh? Wait . . .

"Remembering all we had seen and heard in the vault, and especially Madame Scheffer's frenzied illustration with the goad and pitchfork, we became more and more convinced that these people had gone from pretence to actuality . . . I mean to say, they had carried the reconstruction of the crimes of the 'Inn of Blood' to the finish!

" 'Do you remember,' Maria-Luce said to me, 'do you remember how she stared at the countess?' Here Maria-Luce shivered and went on, 'It was terrifying! One might have believed that the countess was already her prey, chained to the wall like the "pretty little brunette" . . . and that she was scratching her eyes out with the pitchfork! Ah, poor wretches! The ruffians may have tortured her, too, for fifteen days, having already cooked Antonio. And when I think . . . when I think that if it hadn't been for that trouble over the coupé, they would never have played that trick as revenge! . . . It was we who——'

" 'Don't think about it,' I exclaimed. But the matter could not rest there. Maria-Luce had nightmares about it at night, and so did I. At last, to get rid of the obsession, we did our duty. We returned to Soleure, and our first move was to go directly to the police, where we told the whole story from beginning to end.

"An inquest followed which brought immediate results. All the details we gave, all the incidents just as they had happened before our eyes, were confirmed . . . And the Scheffers did not deny a thing. They did not seem in the least fazed by it. And yet there were several questions which might well have embarrassed them; but Scheffer had an answer to everything.

"For example, when the judge asked: 'What did the words Monsieur Chaulieu heard mean: "Which one shall we begin on?" ' he answered quite naturally: 'How do I know? How do you expect me to remember what I said that evening any more than any other evening? My words were of no importance except to the two who thought I was going to murder them. What stupidity! Perhaps they had something to do with the next day's work. I couldn't say . . .'

"But the judge insisted: 'How was it that you and your wife weren't astonished when only two people came down the next morning? Why were you silent about that? We would never have known a thing about all this if Monsieur and Madame Chaulieu had not come themselves to tell us that they fled in the night!'

" 'Why should I be astonished?' Scheffer answered. 'You know the little show we gave and still continue to give for amateurs. It had frightened the little lady, and she can tell you herself that several times during the evening she said: "The whole place frightens me!" No, I was not surprised, and I must admit that we had a good laugh over it when the two Italians told us the next morning, before leaving, that Monsieur and Madame had been frightened to death and had escaped by the attic window . . . Besides, we found the rope there . . . As for the Italians, after the abrupt departure of Monsieur and Madame, they had carried their bedding into the other room and had passed an excellent night there.'

" 'Still, if the incident was as funny as that, you had no reason to keep quiet about it!'

" 'But who told you I did? On the contrary, I've told it scores of times to travellers stopping for a drink . . . But to find them now – '

" 'You might have said something to the stage-driver.'

" 'Oh, when he stops at the inn he has other things to do: he is busy with his horses. Besides, he may have heard my tale, at that.'

" 'No, he has never heard it . . . He never suspected a thing.'

" 'That is quite possible. What should he suspect? . . . That story is a trivial matter. You surprise me with all this fuss.'

" 'The Italians didn't tell you that they frightened Monsieur and Madame in order to obtain possession of the room?'

" 'Good heavens, no.'

"The answer was a serious one, because after all, if the whole thing had only been a joke it was strange that the Italians had not boasted of it before their departure.

" 'I am the only victim in the whole affair,' Scheffer went on, 'because I have not been paid for the bill yet. And that is probably why the Italians did not confess that they were responsible for the flight of the other two: they did not want to be asked to pay for the bill.'

"As you see, he had an answer ready for everything.

"Nevertheless, the judge was perplexed and the inquest continued for some time. They made new searches, but they found nothing and the matter was finally dropped. It was not until three years later, a year after Maria-Luce's death, that the affair came to light again, and this time the papers were full of wild tales.

"Antonio Ferretti and Olivia Orsino had never been heard of again, and you must admit that it was strange. I know that Antonio Ferretti was married and that he may have gone to some far corner of the earth to enjoy his happiness under an assumed name, but, after all, he was just becoming famous, and to give up such a splendid career forever! . . . I grew more and more convinced that they had been murdered, and even today after a lapse of over twenty years I am positive of the fact.

"But I was saying that three years later something new occurred. In excavating not far from the inn, some new bones were found, and you can well picture the stir that it caused. The Weisbachs were on everyone's tongue again. And the Scheffers had become famous overnight, as famous as the Weisbachs had been! The experts, however, did not agree on the age of the bones.

"In the meantime, first one, then two, and then three families who had had disappearances among their relations, claimed that they might quite possibly have been victims of the Scheffers, because they had taken a trip through French Switzerland. They went even so far as to establish the fact that a young man from

Linz, who had abducted a girl of good family, had slept one night at the 'Inn of Blood'. At that, the Scheffers and their servants were arrested and I was called as one of the witnesses.

"Their guilt seemed established and there was no doubt that they would be sentenced, when we suddenly learned that the young man in question had married the young girl of good family in America, and that they were farmers in Minnesota! The Scheffers were acquitted . . . And now my story is done."

"And nothing more was ever heard of the Italians?" Dorat demanded.

"Never."

"And the Scheffers are still going strong?" Captain Michel asked, and this time he was not joking.

"Yes, they are still there making money. I heard of them quite recently from a friend who passed through Soleure. The 'Inn of Blood' has become historical. People come from far and near to see it; only no one ever asks to spend the night in the 'travellers' room'!"

THE WOMAN WITH THE VELVET COLLAR

"You say that all the tales of Corsican vendettas are just the same old story over again," Gobert, a retired sea captain, remarked to his friend Captain Michel. "Well, you're wrong. I know one story that is so terrible that it makes all the others seem mere child's play. It even sent a chill up my hardened spine."

"Yes?" Michel was sceptical. His was the scepticism of a man who, believing himself to have known the most thrilling adventures, does not take stock in other men's tales. "Yes," he went on, "another case of a couple of bullets in the back, I suppose. But go ahead, let's hear it. We haven't anything better to do."

With this last shot, he ordered another round of drinks, and the party of old sea-dogs, who gathered every evening in the Café of the Sea at Toulon to spin their yarns, settled themselves to listen.

"First of all," Gobert began, "my story hasn't anything to do with guns, and secondly, you've never heard of a Corsican vendetta like mine unless, of course, you happened to have been at Bonifacio about thirty years ago, as I was. In that case you would have had your fill of the story because the whole town was agog with it."

He looked around inquiringly, but none of the men present had ever touched at Bonifacio during their many voyages.

"Well, I'm not surprised," Gobert went on. "It's not a port of importance, but it is one of the most picturesque towns in Corsica. You've all seen it, probably, on your way to the Orient. A lovely spot with its old fortress, the turreted battlements, and time-stained walls. The fortress juts out over the crags like an eagle's nest . . ."

"Lay off the descriptions and give us the story," the others exclaimed impatiently.

"All right, here it is. I was in command of a small destroyer forming part of the squadron escorting the Secretary of the Navy on a tour of inspection in Corsica. At that time they were considering the fortification of several ports. In fact, they even thought for a while of turning Porto Vecchio, which is as large as Brest, into a regular naval base.

"The Secretary of the Navy went first to Calvi and Bastia, from where we returned to Ajaccio to wait for him while he crossed the island by train, passing by Vizzavona, where he was met with great ceremony by a delegation of bandits who had left the wilds of the interior that very morning to present their respects to him.

"The famous Bella Coscia himself commanded the squad that fired the salute. The Secretary of the Navy was much impressed with his imposing bearing, his rifle whose carved stock had a nick in it for every man he had killed, and his famous knife – the dagger given to him by Edmond About with the request never to leave it in the wound!"

"There you are, the same old stories," Captain Michel interrupted peevishly. "Just a lot of old wives' tales."

"You're right, old chap; these are just stories, but if you hold your horses, you'll hear something more important.

"We left Ajaccio and arrived in Bonifacio at night. The larger ships continued to Porto Vecchio, but I was among those detailed to escort the Secretary ashore. It was a gala night, of course. A big dinner was followed by a grand reception at the Town Hall.

"Bonifacio, situated as it was opposite Magdalena, wanted fortifications, and its citizens had turned out in great style to make a good impression. They produced the best of everything they had – flowers, finery, and beautiful women, and you know how beautiful Corsican women can be! At dinner there were some striking beauties and I remarked about it enthusiastically to my neighbour, Pietro Santo, a charming fellow of a frank, good-natured appearance, who was then Town Clerk.

" 'Wait until you have seen the woman with the velvet collar,' he said seriously in answer to my remark.

" 'Is she more beautiful than these?' I asked with a smile.

" 'Yes,' he replied without smiling, 'yes, she is more beautiful, but it is not the same kind of beauty . . .'

"In the meantime our conversation drifted to the customs of the country. My head was still ringing with all the brigand stories I had just been hearing from my comrades on their return from escorting the Secretary to Vizzavona, and their account of the spectacular reception by Bella Coscia had seemed to me like a scene from a musical comedy. I thought it was rather polite on my part to doubt the dangerous character of these outlaws. After all, Corsica was as civilised as certain parts of France itself at that time.

" 'The custom of the vendetta,' Santo explained to me after I had spoken, 'continues to be a part of the code of honour here in the same way that duelling is with you. Your revenge accomplished, you automatically find yourself an outlaw. But what can be done about it? It's too bad, of course, but we have to put up with existing facts. I myself am an easygoing man. I was brought up in an antique dealer's shop and I'm sorry to see how savage some of my compatriots still can be when their family honour, as they call it, is in danger.'

" 'You surprise me,' I exclaimed, pointing out to him the jolly, good-natured faces around the banqueting table.

"He shook his head. 'Don't trust them,' he warned, and his face grew dark. 'A laugh changes very quickly to a diabolical grin on their lips. All these dark eyes are sparkling with frankness and merriment tonight. Tomorrow they may flash black with thoughts of hate and revenge. And all those slender, delicate hands clasping each other in good fellowship never cease toying with hidden arms.'

" 'I thought those customs had died out in the cities and only existed in the little villages of the interior,' I said.

" 'The first husband of the lady with the velvet collar was Mayor of Bonifacio, sir.'

"I did not understand the allusion and was on the verge of asking for an explanation of this somewhat enigmatical remark when I was stopped by a call for silence. The speeches were about to begin. At their conclusion we withdrew to the drawing-room, and it was there that I first saw the woman with the velvet collar. Nor did I need Pietro Santo to point her out to me. There was no mistaking that strange funereal beauty and the velvet ribbon, which circled the base of her neck making a wide, black strip against the whiteness of her skin. This velvet collar was worn very low at the rise of the shoulders and emphasised her long and slender neck. She carried her head very proudly, always holding it in a straight, upright position. Her face was classic in its beauty but so pale that one would have believed it chiselled in marble had it not been for two flashing eyes of strange brilliancy.

"As she passed through the room they all bowed to her with lowered eyes and I caught a general atmosphere of fear and instinctive recoil which roused my curiosity to full pitch. Her beautiful body was draped in black velvet and as she came forward, slipping in and out of the crowd, with her proud head and tragically pale face, I had the impression of seeing the dignified ghost of some dead and martyred queen. When she had gone, I turned to my new friend and voiced my feelings about this uncanny woman.

" 'There is nothing strange about that,' he answered seriously. *'She was guillotined!'*

"I looked at him in astonishment. 'What do you mean?' I stammered.

"But he could not answer me immediately. The 'woman with the velvet band', having greeted the Secretary of the Navy, came down the room towards us, stopped and held out her hand to my friend.

" 'Good evening, Pietro Santo,' she said, and I noticed that her head never moved from its rigid position.

"He mumbled something and bowed, and she went on. All the eyes in the room were focused on her and a deep silence had fallen. I noticed then that she was escorted by a handsome, well-built fellow of about thirty. His face had the fine profile often found on old Greek coins. These delicate features are frequently seen among the Corsicans and sometimes give them a family resemblance with the great emperor.

" 'He's her second husband,' Pietro Santo whispered, noticing my gaze.

"The couple disappeared at this moment, and I was conscious of a sigh of relief rising throughout the room, while an old man in a corner crossed himself, muttering a prayer.

" 'They never stay very long,' Pietro Santo explained, 'because they're not on very good terms with the present Mayor, Ascoli. Angeluccia – that is her name – has always been proud and ambitious and she wanted her second husband, Giuseppe Girgenti, to be Mayor like her first one. But they were defeated at the last elections and I think they always will be because of the guillotine affair.'

"I started and caught my friend by the arm. He smiled.

" 'Oh,' he exclaimed, 'you'd like to know the story . . . I hear the Mayor telling it to the Secretary this minute; but he doesn't know it as well as I do . . . You see Captain, I was a member of the household and *I saw everything even to the bottom of the basket*!'

" 'Have a cigar, Santo?' I offered. 'You've never smoked any as good as these.'

"Pietro Santo took a cigar and I fumed with impatience while he chatted with the man who had interrupted us. Afterwards I suggested he come aboard my ship, for I was determined to know the rest of the story before I left Bonifacio."

" 'And so,' I began with a laugh, as soon as we were installed in my cabin, 'you say that woman was guillotined?'

" 'You do wrong to laugh, sir,' he replied, extremely serious. 'She was guillotined and it happened before the eyes of almost all the people you saw this evening. If you noticed, they all crossed themselves when she came into the room.'

"I stared at him in open-eyed amazement and he went on simply: *'That's why she always wears that velvet band: to hide the scar!'*

" 'Mr Santo, you're making fun of me. I'm going to call on Angeluccia and ask her to take off the band before my eyes. I should like to see that scar.'

"The man shook his head. 'She wouldn't take it off, sir. *We all know that if she did her head would fall off.*'

"And so saying, he too made the sign of the cross. I studied him by the light of the little swinging lamp. With his curly hair and slight figure, he looked like a timid angel frightened at the sight of the devil. I could not help smiling.

" 'And yet Antonio Macci, Angeluccia's first husband, was the best of men,' he sighed. 'Who would ever suspect such a thing of him? I loved him, sir. He had been very good to me. He was an antique dealer and had brought me up in his shop. He was famous all through Corsica and known to many tourists to whom he sold souvenirs of Napoleon and the imperial family. He manufactured these curios, because the rage for them was such that the authentic pieces had long been sold and there were no more to be had. He made a fortune in this business, and the tourists were quite happy with their purchases, which they were firmly convinced were authentic. Antonio, however, never lost an opportunity to buy any revolutionary articles when the occasion offered. He was able to sell them at a good price to the English and Americans, who never left the island without first paying him a little visit.

" 'From time to time he made short trips to France to renew our stock, and I went with him the last time he went to Toulon. He had read in the papers that there were some very interesting pieces to be sold at auction and he was anxious to acquire them for his shop.

" 'We made a number of purchases that day. We bought a Bastille relief for 425 francs, General Moreau's bed for 215 francs, Mirabeau's death mask for 1,000 francs, a bezel ring with some locks of Louis XVI's hair for 1,200 francs, and last the famous guillotine which, it seems, Samson himself, the famous executioner, had used. This cost us 921 francs. And we returned home very well pleased with ourselves and our purchases.

" 'We found Angeluccia and her cousin Giuseppe waiting for us on the dock. The Deputy Mayor and a delegation from the Town Council were also waiting for us because Antonio, through his successful business, had become one of the most important men in the town and had been elected Mayor. He was about forty years old at the time and his wife twenty, but this great difference in age did not keep Angeluccia from loving her husband ardently. Giuseppe, however, who was about her age, obviously adored his cousin. Anyone could see it merely by the manner in which he looked at her. But be that as it may, I must add that I for my part had never seen anything in the behaviour of the two to justify the slightest suspicion in the husband. Angeluccia herself was too honest and too upright in her actions to give poor Giuseppe any chance to forget her marital duties. And I never believed that he would have had the daring to attempt such an enterprise. He loved Angeluccia. That was all. And my master knew it as well as the rest of us. Perfectly sure of his wife, he used to joke with her sometimes about it.

" 'Angeluccia, who was kind by nature, asked him to spare her poor cousin and not make too much fun of him because Antonio would never find his equal in imitating and redoing furniture of the Empire and Louis XVI. Giuseppe, in fact, was a real artist. Besides, he knew all of Antonio's business secrets, which was probably why the dealer tolerated a workman who looked at his wife with such eloquent eyes.

" 'Giuseppe's forlorn love made him rather melancholy; but Angeluccia was always gay. She had not yet become the funereal beauty you saw today. She laughed often and was affectionate and happy with her husband like any good little wife who has nothing on her conscience.

" 'Our return was well celebrated. Angeluccia had prepared an excellent luncheon and had invited a few friends to share it with us. Everyone was anxious to hear of the new and sensational purchases and everyone wanted to see them.

" ' "Does the guillotine still work?" one of the guests asked.

" ' "Would you like to try it?" the master of the house answered with a laugh.

" 'During the meal, Antonio, next to whom I was seated, accidentally dropped his napkin and bent over to pick it up. But I had already seen it slide to the floor and my head was under the table at the same time that his was. I straightened up and returned him his napkin. Then with a hurried excuse I left the room, bewildered.

" 'I stumbled into the shop and sank into a chair. My discovery had momentarily stunned me, but as my wits returned to me my first question was: had Antonio seen? No, my sudden movement and the position of my head under the table must have made that impossible. Besides, the very calmness with which he had straightened up and received the napkin from me and the quiet way in which he had resumed conversation should have re-assured me.

" 'I returned to the dining-room, where the meal was finishing gaily. The Deputy Mayor, who is the Mayor today, was insisting on being shown the guillotine immediately. Antonio, however, answered that he must wait until the instrument of death had been put in working order. "I know my Americans," he added with a laugh; "they won't buy it unless it works perfectly!"

" 'Shortly afterwards, the guests took leave of their hosts, and during the rest of the day I could not keep my eyes off An-geluccia, who kissed her husband a hundred times if she kissed him once during the afternoon. It made me shiver to watch her. I did not imagine that such deceit was possible in so young and apparently frank a person.

" 'You see, Captain, when I bent under the table at luncheon I had seen Angeluccia's little foot tightly and amorously pressed between Giuseppe's! Her very movement in releasing her foot had proved the crime to me.

" 'As the days passed, life at the shop went on as usual. A few foreign customers came for the famous guillotine, but the master answered that there were still some necessary repairs and that he would not sell it until it was in perfect working condition. In fact, we were working on it secretly in the basement and had taken it down and put it together several times. It was badly worm-eaten and out of joint and we were trying to balance it properly so that the knife would run smoothly in its grooves. This work revolted me, but it seemed on the contrary to please Antonio.

" 'Angeluccia's birthday and the Pentecost fell on the same date,

and as it was customary for the Mayor to give a party of some sort
on the day of Pentecost, Antonio announced that he had decided
to give a costume ball. This would be an excellent opportunity to
show his guillotine. No one had seen it yet and it was to be the
crowning event of the evening.

" 'Bonifacio is very fond of this sort of amusement, historical
reconstructions and pageants, and when Angeluccia heard the
plan she flung herself on her husband's neck like a happy child.
She herself suggested that she go as Marie Antoinette.

" ' "We'll make it very realistic and guillotine you at the end of
the party," Antonio said with a laugh.

" ' "Why not?" Angeluccia answered. "It would be fun."

" 'When the town knew what sort of a party the Mayor was
planning, everyone wanted to go, and the next fifteen days
before Pentecost were filled with preparations. The shop was full
from morning to night with people running in and out, asking
advice and studying old prints. Antonio was to represent
Fouquier-Tinville, the terrible public accuser. Giuseppe was to
be Samson, the executioner, and I was to fill the humble role of
his aide.

" 'The great day arrived. Early in the morning we emptied the
shop of all the odds and ends with which it was filled and put up
the guillotine. Giuseppe had made a knife of cardboard covered
with silver paper, so that Angeluccia's desire to play the
guillotine scene to the end could be carried out, and we tried the
machine several times to make sure it worked.

" 'We danced all afternoon and at night there was a big ball at
the Town Hall. Everyone drank toast after toast enthusiastically
to the Mayor and his beautiful wife. Angeluccia was dressed in
the costume worn by Marie Antoinette during her imprisonment, and this simple dress, well in keeping with the
feelings of a poor woman destined for so tragic an end, suited her
marvellously. I shall never forget the sight of Angeluccia's
beautiful white neck rising proudly from the delicately crossed
kerchief, and Giuseppe devoured her with his eyes. Catching the
too apparent flame of desire in his look I could not help glancing
from time to time at Antonio, who seemed almost wildly gay.

" 'At the end of the dinner, it was he who gave the signal for the start of the horrible play. In a well-prepared speech, he informed the guests that he and some friends of his had planned a little surprise, which consisted in presenting to them the most tragic hours of the revolution; Bonifacio having the great fortune of possessing a guillotine, they were going to make use of it to decapitate Marie Antoinette.

" 'At these words the people laughed and cheered, giving a merry ovation to Angeluccia, who rose from her seat and declared that she would know how to die courageously as befitted a queen of France.

" 'A roll of drums suddenly beat in the streets, and we ran to the windows. A miserable cart drawn by a dilapidated horse stood there surrounded by guards and officers of the guillotine all wearing the bonnet of the revolution. A group of horrible knitting-women danced and sang in the streets, calling loudly for the death of the Austrian, dethroned queen of France. One might very easily have imagined oneself back in the days of 1793!

" 'We had all taken part in his game without seeing any harm in it, and it wasn't until Angeluccia had stepped into the cart with her hands tied behind her back, and the procession had started to the sinister beat of her funeral drums, that more than one felt a shiver steal up his spine and realised that such a masquerade might well touch upon sacrilege.

" 'The whole scene was horribly effective. Night had fallen, and the flickering light of the torches gave a death-like beauty to Angeluccia's face. And she played her part well. Holding herself proudly erect, she seemed to be braving the populace with her cold stare, and her face with its changeless severity of expression might well have been carved in stone.

" 'We reached Antonio's house, and there the gay laughs broke out anew. Antonio was already in the shop, where he had seated a chosen group of people who were to watch the mock execution. The mob was thickly packed in, and everyone was in a state of extreme excitement at finally seeing the famous guillotine at such a close range. My master asked for silence and began by making a little speech on the good points of his instrument of death. He mentioned all the noble necks which, he claimed, had rested on the head-boards, and he ended by exhibiting the real knife which he had bought at the same time.

" ' "I had the paper knife up there made so that you could see just how the thing worked," he explained; then, turning to Giuseppe, "Are you ready, Samson?"

" 'Samson replied that he was ready.

" ' "Bring forth the Austrian," Antonio ordered in a deep voice.

" 'Giuseppe and I placed Marie Antoinette – Angeluccia – on the plank, and Antonio himself lowered the board that held her head in position.

" 'The laughter in the room suddenly ceased and an uneasy feeling swept over the crowd. The sight of the lovely body stretched out on the plank brought to the minds of even the hardened men present the memory of all the unfortunates who had really lain there to die. The joke had been carried too far. The merriment was revived for the moment, however, by the sight of Angeluccia's amused face as she looked here and there at the guests while her husband finished his lecture on the machine, showing the basket which received the body and that into which the head fell.

" 'But suddenly, as we watched Angeluccia an awful change came over her face. Wild terror was written there. Her eyes had widened horribly and her mouth opened as though to let out a cry which stuck in her throat.

" 'Giuseppe was at the back and had seen nothing of this; but I, who was at the side, was struck with a nameless fear as the others had been. We were looking at the sight of one who really *knew* she was going to be decapitated. The laughter had died out and some of the people even shrank back as though struck by an invincible terror.

" 'As for me, I came closer, for I had suddenly noticed that Angeluccia's horror-stricken eyes were staring at something in the bottom of the basket which was to receive the head. I looked into this basket, which Antonio had opened only a moment before, and I too read what Angeluccia had read – I too read the little placard fastened to the bottom:

Pray to the Virgin Mary, Angeluccia, wife of Antonio, mistress of Giuseppe, for you are about to die!

" 'I uttered a hollow cry and turned like a madman to stop Giuseppe, who, at a motion from Antonio, had seized the rope. Alas! I was too late. The knife fell, and what followed was horrible, too horrible for words. The unfortunate woman let out a scream which ended in an abrupt gurgle – a scream which will echo in my ears to my dying day – and then her blood spouted out over the audience, who let out sickening cries and made a desperate fight for the door. I fainted.'

"Here Pietro Santo stopped and grew so pale at the memory of the awful scene that I feared he was going to be ill. I restored some of his strength with a glass of old grappa.

" 'But in spite of all that,' I said to him, 'Angeluccia was not killed. I saw her myself and she certainly was alive.'

"He sighed and lifted his head.

" 'Are you sure she really is alive?' he asked. 'There isn't a soul in Bonifacio who passes her in the street without crossing himself. Seeing her never look to the right nor to the left, always holding her head rigid, they firmly believe that her head is held to her neck by some supernatural miracle. That is how the legend of the velvet collar grew. Besides, she looks like a ghost, and when she shakes hands with me the touch of her icy skin makes me tremble.

" 'Yes, I know it's childish, but the whole affair was such a strange one you must excuse the fantastic tales which our peasant folk have created. The truth of the matter is, I suppose, that Antonio planned his blow badly, that the machine was too old and did not work properly, and that Angeluccia's head was pushed too far through the opening, in such a way that the knife struck her at the rise of the shoulders. This is not the first time that such an accident has occurred with the guillotine. We have heard of cases where it took five tries to cut the head off. Giuseppe was the only one present when the doctor, whom he himself had fetched, saw her, and he says the wound was quite large. Everybody ran away at the time, and Antonio himself disappeared. You can see how all this helped form the legend that grew up overnight. Even those who were present at the time claim that they saw Angeluccia's head actually drop into the basket!

" 'Naturally, when Angeluccia reappeared some weeks later with the velvet ribbon, imaginations ran riot. And even when I look at her, there are times when I am hypnotised by her neck and wouldn't dare *under any circumstances untie her velvet band*!'

" 'And what happened to Antonio?'

" 'He is dead, or at least so they say. At any rate, his decease has been legally published since Giuseppe and Angeluccia are married. They found his body half eaten by crabs on the beach near the grottoes. The corpse was completely disfigured, but they found papers on it and the clothes were his. He probably ran away, believing Angeluccia dead, and threw himself over the cliff. He had prepared his revenge well, silently and cunningly as they do here, but I am still amazed at the skill with which he hid his feelings from the day that he first got an inkling of the truth of the relations between Angeluccia and her cousin.

" 'The police have the duplicate knife that he made so that it would look like Giuseppe's. It is in Ajaccio.' "

"Your story isn't bad," Captain Michel conceded generously to Gobert. "It has an element of horror in it."

"It's not finished yet," Gobert explained, asking for another few minutes of silence. "Let me go on and you will see that it really is horrible. I didn't know the end myself until some time later on a second voyage to Bonifacio, and it was good old Pietro Santo who related the concluding details to me.

"Imagine my extreme amazement when on asking him news of the woman with the velvet collar, he answered me in perfect seriousness: 'Captain, the legend was right after all. *Angeluccia died on the day that the velvet collar was touched!*'

" 'What!' I cried. 'But who undid the collar?'

" '*I did. And her head fell off!*'

"While I stared at Pietro Santo, wondering if he had lost his mind, he explained to me that after I had left Bonifacio a doubt had spread through the town as to the truth of Antonio's supposed death. It seemed that Ascoli, the Mayor, was responsible for this and claimed to know what he was talking about. He was convinced that he had met Antonio one day when he was out hunting. The man had been almost naked, living like a wild beast, and when Ascoli tried to speak to him he ran away.

"It was during this time that the elections for Mayor came up again and Giuseppe was Ascoli's rival for the post. During the entire campaign, Ascoli declared that Giuseppe was the accomplice of a bigamous woman and therefore unworthy of the position. Giuseppe's rage knew no bounds when he was defeated and he resolved to hunt Antonio out. It took him several months to do so, but he finally accomplished his purpose. Antonio, who for ten years had never spoken to a soul, learned that his wife was not dead as he had supposed but was living happily with Giuseppe in the very house in which he had been Mayor and had believed himself loved by her.

" 'What happened then,' Pietro Santo went on in a hollow voice, 'is beyond conception, and would make even the demons in hell shrink in horror. Good Lord, if I live to be a thousand . . . But to cut it short, sir, the story can be told in a few words.

" 'One evening, a soft, clear evening like this, I was returning from an expedition to the grottoes, where I had escorted some friends, and was seated in the little boat taking us back to port when, in passing the cliffs, I heard a chant that made my blood run cold. It was the song which is always sung here by those who have some mortal affront to avenge. I lifted my head. A man stood like a statue on the edge of the rocks which served as a sort of pedestal to him. Although he was dressed in rags, he shouldered his gun proudly, and suddenly, as the last rays of the sun caught his face and brought it into full relief, I uttered one cry: "Antonio!"

" 'It was he! It was he! Oh, I was sure it was he! His fatal song and exalted air convinced me that he had not returned to these parts, after playing dead for ten years, without nursing some abominable purpose.

" 'Fortunately, I could reach town quicker by boat than he could on foot. There would be time to warn Giuseppe and Angeluccia. I threw myself on the oars and reached the dock in a few minutes. The first person I met was Giuseppe himself, who was on his way home from the Town Hall. I thanked heaven I had arrived in time and called out to him to hurry, that a terrible misfortune was about to fall, that I had seen Antonio – Antonio himself – alive, and that he was on his way to town.

" 'While questioning me he fell into step beside me and we both ran for his house at full speed and arrived there panting.

" ' "Angeluccia! Angeluccia!" we called, flinging open the door.

" 'No answer.

" ' "God help us if she's gone for a walk," Giuseppe groaned desperately.

" 'We went upstairs, still calling her, and he went into one room while I entered another. And it was there that I found her. She was seated by the window in a large armchair, her head resting against the cushion, and she seemed to be sleeping. As she was always extremely pale, the pallor of her beautiful face did not surprise me although it might have struck another.

" ' "Come," I cried to Giuseppe, "she is here."

" 'In the meantime I had come closer, surprised that she did not awake. I touched her . . . I touched the velvet band, which came loose in my hands, *and her head rolled off!*

" 'I fled with my heart pounding wildly from shock and fright, but on my way I slipped and fell in a horrible pool of blood, which I had not noticed on entering because of the shadows which darkened the room. I picked myself up with a yell and left the house madly. People ran from me in the streets as one runs from a wild beast.

" 'During the next few days I came near to going insane. Fortunately I completely recovered my senses, well enough, in fact, to be the present Mayor of Bonifacio. As you probably understand by now, sir, I had seen Antonio *as he was returning from the deed!* It was easy enough to figure the whole thing out then. He had entered the house, found Angeluccia alone, and killed her with a stab in the heart. Then, his mind haunted by what Ascoli had told him, he completed the work which he had commenced so clumsily ten years before. More certain of his Corsican dagger than of the mock-historical instrument which had failed him before, he had decapitated her and without shrinking from the atrocity of the deed had *replaced her head on her shoulders and had tied it in position with the velvet ribbon*!

" 'And now,' concluded Pietro Santo, 'if you want news of Giuseppe you will have to go into the wilds for it. Two days after the murder, he disappeared into the mountains with a gun over his shoulder and Angeluccia's head, which he had embalmed himself, in a sack around his waist. Giuseppe, Ascoli and Antonio have never been seen since, but they have probably met in the approved fashion and killed each other in some hidden corner of the woods.

" 'That, sir, is the only way in which the custom of vendetta will be done away with in this country: when everybody is dead!' "

THE CRIME ON CHRISTMAS NIGHT

FIVE OLD SKIPPERS smelling of the sea used to foregather every evening at one of the round tables in front of the old Ship and Anchor Café in Toulon to enjoy their aperitifs and at the same time to tell each other stories of blood and horror. From time to time they were joined by a sixth who seemed to be more of an old sea-dog even than Zinzin, he who had spent twenty years coasting up and down the China Seas; than Dorat, the ex-commander of the Dorat expeditions; than Bagatelle, who, in memory of a blissful sojourn on the Island of Siam, had taken a Siamese woman unto wife; than that blackguard Chaulieu, who had carried the benefits of civilisation to the aborigines of Western Africa, settled between the Congo and the Niger; than Captain Michel, who knew about cannibalism and some mariners who had passed several weeks on a raft of the *Medusa*, from which the shipwrecked had escaped with their lives, even though some were minus an arm, others a leg, and all more or less crippled.

This sixth "mariner", Mr Damour (John-Joseph-Philibert), had gained his entire nautical experience seated at his desk in the offices of the Oriental Transportation Company, and he used to refer in an offhand way to the far-flung Pacific ports of call as we lesser men might speak, say, of some pleasant little fishing cove along the Seine.

To tell the truth, he had never set foot on the deck of a ship, nor had he even been outside Paris except on the day when he retired. But his face was so weather-beaten, his skin so tough, his beard so rebellious, his clay pipe so stubby and so "seasoned", his walk so typically the sailor's sway, that you had only to glance at him and you would exclaim, "There's one who's weathered many a gale."

He whetted the curiosity of the old salts and they made him welcome when on one unusually crowded day at the café he lifted his Basque beret and asked if he might have a seat at their table. He came again from time to time and it took them some months to grasp the idea that John-Joseph (this was what they called Mr Damour), who from the beginning made himself known to them as captain, had really never been on any voyage anywhere.

The old fellow used to give such precise details concerning the most distant parts of the globe, setting every one straight who erred on any point; he was so glib with facts about the history of liners from their christening day to the day of their sometimes very dramatic end, that for a long time the skippers kept their doubts to themselves. But on the day when the truth did come out there was the devil to pay! It was their turn now, and it goes without saying that they gave it to him hammer and tongs for the deception. And yet there was one thing they could not figure out at all, and that was how, after thirty years spent behind a desk in a sunless steamship office, scribbling figures in piles of paper, a man could still have a face like "Captain" John-Joseph. "It must be he makes himself up for the part," declared Captain Michel. And Zinzin re-echoed, "Yeah, he trims up like that over at the 'Black Lion'."

Quite a time passed and he didn't come around. Finally he showed up with a young man of about twenty who really did sail the seas and no mistaking it. But he didn't think it was anything to boast about; he was as pale as a girl, and he admitted quite frankly that he'd never yet made a trip without being seasick. "He's my adopted son, young Vincent Vincent, a real sailor," John-Joseph told his friends, proudly.

Every time Vincent Vincent's ship docked at Toulon, John-Joseph was so happy about it that it wasn't unusual to see him come into the café rolling and pitching more than ever; three sheets in the wind, no less! He had probably drunk as much liquor as any three dozen hearty sailors could hold.

"For the love o' God," said that devil of a Chaulieu, "where've you been, John-Joseph, to get such a load on?"

"Just come from seeing the boy off from Marseilles,"

answered John-Joseph in a very sentimental tone, as he began to blubber.

"Well, if you feel so bad about it and it's no fun for the boy," suggested Captain Michel, "there are plenty of other jobs he could take."

"No, he couldn't," replied John-Joseph emphatically, as he gulped down another glassful.

Not one of the company contradicted him; they all agreed with him on that point at least.

"And then," he added, "I don't want to have the day come when they'll take it out on him, poor lad, as they tried to do out of his adopted father."

At this point he began to cry, and he sobbed as can only very drunken men when great sorrows overwhelm them.

"Come on, now, tell us the truth," asked Bagatelle, his sexual imagination always alert; "are you really that boy's father?"

"No," John-Joseph answered bluntly, tears streaming down his cheeks. "No, I'm not his father . . . His father was murdered!"

"The poor boy," said Zinzin, just to say something.

"Yes, the poor boy . . . because I was just going to tell you, his mother . . ."

"What's that? His mother?" Bagatelle pricked up his ears.

"Well, his mother, she was murdered too!"

"Oh, for the love o' God!" exclaimed Bagatelle.

"That," said Zinzin, "that's a horrible story."

"More horrible than any I've heard you fellows tell," stuttered John-Joseph between his hiccups.

"Well, you've got to show us," said Captain Dorat; "for, after all, one of the reasons we come here every day it to listen to tales of horror."

"It isn't more terrible than what happened to Captain Michel," declared Zinzin.

"I say it is – only you mustn't tell it to anyone. It's a secret," puffed out John-Joseph, trying to swallow a second hiccup.

"Stop your sniffling," commanded Michel, "and tell us all about it. You'll feel better when it's out of your system."

"Not to mention that that happens every day," said Chaulieu

rather scornfully, "to have your father and mother murdered – I don't see anything very terrible about that. Who murdered them?"

John-Joseph wiped his eyes with his big red bandanna handkerchief and hiccuped: "Wasn't any murderers."

"How can that be? They were murdered but nobody murdered them?"

"That's just what's so terrible," sighed John-Joseph. "The poor wretches were found stabbed with a kitchen knife – a real butchery. The old man's blood was dripping all over the carpet and the knife was still sticking in the old woman's heart."

"So they'd been fighting?"

"Fighting!" flared up John-Joseph, looking round at the company. "Those two good people? Easy to see you never knew them. They were the kind of married folks who never spoke a cross word to each other in their lives, and they weren't going to begin on that day, I'll have you know. I'm the only one that can give my word of honour to that too. No, they were murdered after there'd been a robbery."

"Now then, why did you first say there weren't any murderers when it was the thieves that murdered them?"

"Wasn't any thieves," John-Joseph cut off short.

"Good God," said Chaulieu.

"Oh, let him go to hell," grunted Dorat.

"Give him a chance to tell his own story," ordered Captain Michel.

"I've got no more to say," declared John-Joseph.

This time all five burst into shouts of laughter. Seeing which, John-Joseph became raging angry. Now he really wanted to tell his story and as the others kept on making fun of him he thumped so hard on the table that he scattered the stacked-up saucers right and left and bellowed, "I swear that in a few minutes you won't be making fun."

"All right, then, come on now, we're all listening."

John-Joseph began: "At that time, my home port was Germain-Pilon Street – "

"Paris-on-the-sea," teased Chaulieu.

"Damn it all, I'll not say another word until that big pig gets to hell out of here."

"Don't worry, John-Joseph, you couldn't hire me to stay," answered Chaulieu. "I'm going to take a turn about," and he rose. " 'The horrible murder in Germain-Pilon Street' . . . very little of that goes a long way with me. I'd rather spend my time looking at the pretty women on the screen over at the Palace."

When he had gone, John-Joseph went on:

"I don't know if any of you fellows know Germain-Pilon Street. It climbs from the avenue up to the top of Montmartre. It's a lonely neighbourhood – not always many people about. But the street is respectable enough. There's where I came to know the Vincent family. They were what you call 'comfortably off' and their friends were even rather surprised to see them keep on living in a section thought rather dangerous; but they said that in the fifteen years they had lived there nothing had ever happened to them and they'd rather live in a little house with a back yard and a garden all to themselves than in a big apartment house where you had to knock against all the other tenants every time you turned around.

"I was their neighbour, and although they weren't very sociable, we got acquainted through the little baby. He was a sweetheart of a child and I spoiled him every time I could . . . I've always adored children . . . One Christmas night – "

"Hell, one of those Christmas stories!" groaned Zinzin. "Well, see you later, boys."

And he went out to join Chaulieu.

"Got anything about a woman in your Christmas story?" Bagatelle asked.

"Yes."

"Good – go on then."

"One Christmas night, Madame Vincent, in her felt slippers, came downstairs to the dining-room where her husband sat toasting his feet at the fireplace waiting for her.

" 'Is the baby sleeping?' Monsieur Vincent asked.

" 'Like an angel,' answered the good woman.

"They adored that child born after they had been married many years. His arrival so late in their lives filled them with an almost supernatural joy. Madame Vincent was forty-five when this happiness came to her, and her husband fifty-five. One sees miracles like that every once in a while.

"Theirs was a perfect marriage; up to this time they had lived just for each other. From now on they lived only for that little child. They baptised him Vincent, and as their family name was also Vincent, the neighbours used to say when they saw the baby go by in his mother's arms:

" 'There he is, the darling; there's little Vincent Vincent and his mama going for a turn on the avenue.' "

"And I too," declared Captain Dorat, as he rose to leave.

Bagatelle tried to dissuade him.

"Wait a minute until he gets to the part about the woman," he said to Dorat.

"Ah, to hell with his story – John-Joseph's a bore. He's not even drunk any more now."

"John-Joseph, give me your word of honour that the part about the woman is worth waiting for," demanded Bagatelle.

"I swear," John-Joseph declared, "that it's impossible to find anything more horrible."

"And is there any love in your story?"

"Is there? – love even unto death. But if you're sensitive you'd better go now; for such a death – well, you don't see them often in love stories."

"I stay," Bagatelle decided. But Dorat had already left to join the other two.

The memory of little Vincent Vincent's happy babyhood completely sobered John-Joseph. He even forgot to keep his old clay pipe alight. From now on he told his story in the style of the former model employee.

"I don't need to tell you how Papa and Mama Vincent allowed themselves to spoil their baby in a thousand loving ways – cakes, candies, toys, ice-creams, little suits of velvet and lace. They were his adoring slaves – nothing was too beautiful, nothing cost too much for little Vincent.

"The couple had been employed in the well-known shop, 'Smart Styles', ever since that house had been established, and at the time of their baby's coming they were earning, with their bonuses and all, on an average of 20,000 francs a year, which permitted them to lay by a nice little nest egg.

"After Vincent's birth, although they never thought twice about spending right and left for him, they began to deprive themselves of all the little indulgences that had up to now made their married life so sweet. They counted every penny; little by little they became even miserly. No more anniversary dinners; no more visits to the theatre; no more Sunday excursions into the country; no more pleasant evening parties, playing games with their friends. All that would be so much put away for the little angel who would find it when he needed it.

"After he had prayed the Infant Jesus to put a beautiful present in the little shoes he had set purposely in front of the dining-room fireplace, little Vincent had fallen off to sleep on this Christmas night, knowing his parents were to wake him up later to see the lighted Christmas tree.

"The sight of those little shoes on the hearth must have been very touching, for Mama Vincent noticed that when Papa Vincent saw them there his eyes filled with tears. She went up to him and patted him on the shoulder.

" 'Come now, Papa Vincent, you're not going to cry on Christmas night, I hope.'

"He got up from his chair. 'I can't help it,' he stammered. 'I've never been able to look at those little baby shoes showing where his little toes have been, without a lump in my throat. I know it's silly. Forgive me, my dear wife.'

" 'Do I forgive you?' and as she said it, she drew him to her bosom and kissed him with all the tenderness of a first kiss. Then when she felt herself also yielding to emotion she straightened up, wiped away a tear with the back of her hand and said:

" 'Come now, Papa Vincent, lend a hand. We're going to trim the Christmas tree.'

" 'So we are. Let's make it gay and beautiful for him, all pink and shining when he opens his eyes on it, the little dear.' "

Bagatelle burst forth with, "For the love o' God, you don't forget anything do you? But how do you know they did all that? You weren't there, were you?"

"Papa Vincent told me all these little things, understand?"

"No," insisted Bagatelle. "I don't understand, if it's the night he was murdered."

"It's the very night," and John-Joseph's voice was getting more and more dismal.

"Well then?"

"Well, he told me after he'd been murdered."

"You're pretty slick, you always put us in the wrong. But for God's sake, get on to the part about the woman. Afterwards, we will see."

"All right; listen then," began John-Joseph.

"Every year since the coming of the baby, they had set up a Christmas tree after supper in the dining-room and trimmed it with all the toys and all the little gifts they had bought. When they finished trimming, they used to go out for a walk, and drop into church for the midnight mass. Then they would come back home, light the pink candles, go upstairs to the baby whom the maid had been watching, lift him up gently and wake him up only when they stood right in front of the tree all dressed with glittering tinsel and stars to make the child happy. They did the very same thing this year as ever.

"That night, there was a travelling fair set up on the avenue; tents had been put up along the pavement and in empty spaces. It was a fine mild evening; winter had hardly set in, and the men and women drinking their beer in the open air in front of the cafés lingered to look at the dancers and listen to the catchy tunes of the merry-go-rounds and hurdy-gurdies."

"Did Papa Vincent tell you all this after he'd been murdered?"

"Yes, everything."

"He must have had an awful thirst!"

"I gave him something to drink," said John-Joseph, "and then he drew his last breath – "

"Before he had proposed another round of drinks?"

"No, but after he had entrusted his little son to me."

"But what about that woman, for God's sake?"

"I'm coming to her."

Calm now, John-Joseph took up the thread of his story.

"Madame and Monsieur Vincent went up to Place Blanche, where they met some very old friends, the Duponts, who wanted to stop for a little chat. But after the barest how-do-you-do, the Vincents left the Duponts and walked rapidly down to the Church of the Holy Trinity, where they intended to listen to the midnight mass."

It was now Captain Michel's turn to get up.

"Where are you going?" Bagatelle asked him.

"My religious scruples," the captain explained good-naturedly, "Keep me from going to Holy Trinity for the midnight mass. You must excuse me, John-Joseph. I belong to the re-formed church."

"Oh, you damned old infidel!" pleaded Bagatelle. "Wait at least till he gets to the part where the woman comes in."

"A damned old infidel," said the captain, mock-seriously, "takes no pleasure whatever in stories about women . . . not even good women," he added, and wished the company good-night.

Bagatelle was now the only one left to listen. John-Joseph went right on. Even if his stack of saucers had been his only audience, he would have gone right along. He couldn't stop now; his own story fascinated him. It was the first time he had ever told it and it would probably be the last. He wanted to prove to himself that he too could tell a story of horror.

"After the Vincents left them, the Duponts swore they were ill-bred, declaring they had never been friendly and sociable since the birth of their baby.

"Reaching the church, the Vincents went in, even though they had a whole hour to wait before the services began. They walked right straight up to the cradle and knelt upon the steps before the

Infant Jesus lying there in the manger between the ox and the ass.

" 'He looks just like our baby,' whispered Papa Vincent. But his wife paid no attention to him. She was buried so deeply and so passionately in prayer that the lights and the organ and the crowd elbowing past her couldn't make her turn her head. When the mass was over, her husband had to lay his hand gently on her shoulder to bring her back out of that pious stupor. When she turned to look at him, her face was like wax.

" 'Heavens,' he said, 'it's not good for you to pray like that. Come, I'm sure our boy is already awake and watching for us to come back.'

" 'Yes, yes,' she said, 'let's hurry along.'

"And she led him on as though she was really trying to flee something. He had difficulty in keeping up with her. He was all out of breath when they reached the avenue, and he tried to make her slow up a little.

" 'No, not yet,' she said. 'We must get back as quick as ever we can.'

"He thought she was afraid to be out in the streets of that district at such a late hour. As a matter of fact, that corner of Paris had never been more disquieting. The hurdy-gurdies had ceased groaning out their tirra-lirras. A few melancholy lights trembled down in the deserted avenue, and behind suspicious shadows, pleasure-seeking gentlemen eyed belated girls wandering up and down the streets.

"However, the Vincents did get back home safe and sound. As soon as they were in their dining-room with the lamp lighted, the sight of the bright Christmas tree drove out of their heads all the ugly sight of the streets. From the foot of the staircase, Monsieur Vincent called to the maid, softly, so as not to wake up the child, but she didn't answer. Just as he started to go up, Madame Vincent said:

" 'She dropped off to sleep beside Vincent. Don't disturb her; let's finish arranging everything here.'

"Then, in great excitement, they put the last touches to the tree. They tied some more toys to the branches already weighted down with Punch and Judy boxes; they hung some dolls and some mechanical toys and some games they had bought from time to time during the year and laid away for this very moment. Papa Vincent was just getting ready to slip a general and his trumpet into the little shoes on the hearth when Mama Vincent stopped him short and said:

" 'No, no, not in the shoes. Don't put anything in the shoes. I'll take care of them!'

"And she spread a napkin on the table, put some glasses on it, some plates and some little cakes, and brought out a bottle of champagne. Then she lit the little rose candles on the tree. It was a real illumination. You've never seen anything gayer, prettier than that room all trimmed up in red and silver. The only thing lacking to start the party was baby Vincent himself.

" 'I'll go upstairs and wake him up,' said his mother. 'You wait for us down here.'

" 'And the shoes? Are you forgetting the shoes?' asked the father.

" 'No, I'm not forgetting them. It's a surprise; you shall see.'

" 'Good . . . all right.'

"She disappeared for a second into the kitchen and took from a case an object which she hid quickly under the cloak she hadn't taken off since they had come back from the mass.

" 'Ha, ha, I caught you at it, sly one,' laughed Monsieur Vincent. 'Come, let me see the surprise too; show it to me.'

" 'Go along with you; you're more of a child than little Vincent. Go back to the dining-room. I want you to, my dear.'

"It was always his way to do everything she told him to. He went back and sat down again in front of the Christmas tree. As for her, she hurried to the floor above.

"She ran up the stairs so fast that she had to stop a moment on the landing. Her heart beat so furiously it almost choked her. On her right hand was the half-open door of the room where little Vincent lay sleeping; on the left a closed door leading to their own bedroom. Before this one she stopped, drew a key from her pocket, unlocked the door, closed it behind her and found herself in pitch blackness. Feeling her way along, she came to the fireplace, kicking to right and left the objects she stumbled on. At last her fingers touched a box of matches; she struck one; she found a candle and lighted up the room.

"Suddenly the flickering light of the candle revealed a terrible disorder. Sheets and mattresses snatched from the bed lay strewn across the floor; night table and centre table were turned upside down; toilet objects had been smashed, a mirrored wardrobe completely ransacked, the clothes thrown here, there and everywhere; several window-panes had been shivered into a thousand pieces. Finally she noticed the sticky, black traces of old slippers by whose aid someone had tried to muffle his footsteps – for the room had certainly been the scene of a robbery.

"The candlelight, flickering and leaping in the breeze blowing in through the window, added weird shadows to the fantastic horror of that scene of devastation.

"To leave the warm atmosphere of the Christmas celebration, of the soft enchantment of that room below where everything is prepared for the sweetest and purest of family joys and to wake up suddenly in the midst of that icy fear – wasn't that more than enough to congeal forever the simple heart of good Madame Vincent? In any case, even if that heart did still beat after such a shock, what inexpressible anguish must have seized little Vincent's mother when she thought of her baby asleep only two steps from that tragic spot, devastated as pitiably as though a tornado had raged through it!

"Well, no . . . Madame Vincent, walking so cautiously in the midst of that disorder, the candle in one hand and a knife in the other – a huge kitchen knife quite new, the mysterious object she was hiding under her cloak a little while ago – Madame Vincent showed neither surprise nor fear."

"She knew there had been a robbery and she had kept it from her husband so as not to spoil the Christmas party," broke in Bagatelle, who was not at all lacking in common sense.

"But I've already told you there had been no robbery."

"You've gone daft and I'm going crazy . . . well, never mind; but what about that woman? What did she have to do with all this business?"

"Everything. She was the one who committed the robbery."

"Good God! My head's cracking open with your damn story. All right . . . go on. When she saw what had happened what did she do, old woman Vincent?"

"She went into little Vincent's room; she woke up the dozing maid; she sent her up to her own room to finish off her night's sleep. Then there was little Vincent who opens his pretty blue eyes in his mother's arms. He doesn't cry. He knows it's Christmas. He's been dreaming about it. He wakes up with the idea of all the gifts waiting for him downstairs. He claps his little hands together and gurgles, 'Christmas, Christmas', and the kisses he bites from his mama's cheeks taste as sweet to him as though they were chocolate nougats.

"The little angel is as happy as he can be. He stretches out his arms towards the sparkling Christmas tree. He wants to touch everything, take everything in his hands, play with everything at the same time. His papa and mama can hardly seem to keep him satisfied.

"Then all of a sudden his merry eyes fall on his little shoes on the hearth. He sees they are empty. He begins to cry.

"Papa Vincent looks reproachfully at Mama Vincent. 'Why did you make him unhappy?' he asks. But Mama takes her little one in her arms; she consoles him, cuddles him, dries his tears.

" 'Little Jesus didn't want to bring everything to you tonight. Little Jesus will come again tomorrow morning. Tomorrow morning there will be some beautiful presents in little Vincent's shoes.'

" 'Will there truly, Mama?'

" 'I promise you there will be, my darling baby.'

"His mother's words bring smiles of joy back to Vincent's eyes again.

" 'But what surprise are you keeping back from him?' asked the father in a low voice.

" 'You shall see, you shall see,' Mama answers with an air of mystery.

"And Mama Vincent takes her good husband's head, draws it down to the baby's and covers both of them with big, passionate kisses and silent tears. This demonstration, so unexpected and somewhat nervous, makes Papa Vincent a little anxious.

" 'You frighten me,' he whispers to his wife.

" 'Let's eat some supper,' she answers.

"And they sit down quietly to their supper and she pours out the champagne and the child is allowed to dip his lips in the foam. Then, his arms still grasping the toys, he dozes off to sleep again on his father's knee.

" 'Carry him back up to his little crib,' says Mama. 'Stay with him a few minutes to be sure he drops back to sleep. I'll go and put out the candles on the tree and then I'll come up to bed.'

"Papa Vincent does as she tells him. Mama Vincent blows out all the candles quickly. Now all is dark where a few minutes before the Christmas tree was glittering and pink. By the feeble rays of the light coming from Vincent's room, she climbs the stairs. Her legs tremble under the weight of her body and she holds on to the banister as though she were afraid she would fall backwards. She sighs with relief when she reaches the landing.

" 'What's the matter with you?' her husband asks in a low voice from the boy's bedroom.

"But Mama Vincent doesn't answer. She is too weak to speak. She turns her eyes away from her son's crib. She pushes open the door of the ransacked room. She ploughs through the disorder; she lights a candle. Once again her eyes take in the sickening horror of it all.

"She grasps the knife – the big, new, shiny kitchen knife, so finely sharpened – and she places herself behind the door.

"Her husband calls out to her from the other room; he gets no answer.

"He appears, his broad chest well lighted by the reddish light of the sputtering candle flame. He asks: 'Why don't you answer, my de – '

"But he is not able to finish the word.

"Mama Vincent stretched forth her arm and struck two terrible blows. The man uttered a shriek and fell down. But she threw herself upon him and covered his mouth with her hand.

" 'Be quiet . . . don't speak.'

" 'Ah, it's you,' he said through his struggling breath. 'It's you.'

" 'Yes, it is I. Don't speak.'

"Between two snatches of breath the man has enough strength to say: 'At least, shut – the door.'

"She drags herself to the door, closes it again and comes back to the big, bleeding body which she now stares at with eyes full of tears and terror.

" 'My dear, my dear wife,' sighs the wretched man, 'you did right. But are you sure everything is well thought out? Will there by any suspicions?'

"No, no, no one will suspect anything.' And she stretched herself out beside him and pressed her lips upon her victim's.

" 'Don't you forgive me?'

" 'Of course I forgive you. You had – more courage than I had.'

" 'Don't say that. But if I had let you do it you would have killed yourself and they would have known that you were a suicide. I made believe a robbery.'

" 'You did right – yes – it was complete ruin – worse than I told you the night before last. The business utterly wiped out . . . not a penny left . . . manager fled . . . all the employees' savings squandered. You have done just right, my dear wife.'

"He closed his eyes and said nothing more. She thought he was dead. Carefully she drew the knife out of the horrible wound. Then his eyelids moved once more.

" 'What are you doing?' he asked with one breath.

" 'Nothing.'

" 'Don't touch it,' he said again, 'don't touch the knife.'

" 'Be quiet, my dear. They would, you understand, ask me some questions. I must not be – able to answer. They must think we've been murdered – both of us . . . you understand? Vincent – if possible, don't die before I do – wait, wait. Here, let me have your hand – help me – do that little thing for me – help me – Vincent. There – like that – strong – ah ah!'

"Helped by Vincent's hand, she buried the knife in her

heart – deliberately – steadily – and as she died she whispered:
'My little boy, Vincent, one hundred thousand francs in – your
little shoes.' "

John-Joseph ceased. Bagatelle looked at him more stunned
than terror-struck. "How's that?" he said; "what did she mean,
one hundred thousand francs in the little shoes?"

John-Joseph began to blubber again. "Father Vincent didn't
die till the next day. He had time to explain to me that he would
not have been able to pay the premium on the life insurance he
had taken out in favour of his little son. They were both too old to
take up some new kind of work. In this way they were sure that
little Vincent would never want for anything."

Bagatelle didn't feel like joking any more. "So, then, the
woman in the story, she's Mama Vincent?"

"Exactly," replied John-Joseph. "Have you ever seen a couple
who loved each other like that?"

"Oh, pooh," answered Bagatelle, shaking his head. "It's a
damn good love story – I won't say no to that – but nobody
would ever say there was anything very horrible about it."

IN LETTERS OF FIRE

WE HAD BEEN out hunting wild boars all day, when we were overtaken by a violent storm, which compelled us to seek refuge in a deep cavern. It was Makoko, our guide, who took upon himself to give utterance to the thought which haunted the minds of the four of us who had sought safety from the fury of the tempest – Mathis, Allan, Makoko, and myself.

"If the gentleman who lives in yonder house, which is said to be haunted by the devil, does not grant us the shelter of his roof tonight, we shall be compelled to sleep here."

Hardly had he uttered the words when a strange figure appeared at the entrance to the cavern.

"It is *he*!" exclaimed Makoko, grasping my arm.

I stared at the stranger.

He was tall, lanky, of bony frame, and melancholy aspect. Unconscious of our presence, he stood leaning on his fowling piece at the entrance of the cavern, showing a strong aquiline nose, a thin moustache, a stern mouth, and lacklustre eyes. He was bareheaded; his hair was thin, while a few grey locks fell behind his ears. His age might have been anywhere between forty and sixty. He must have been strikingly handsome in the days when the light still shone in those time-dimmed eyes and those bitter lips could still break into a smile – but handsome in a haughty and forbidding style. A kind of terrible energy still lurked beneath his features, spectral as those of an apparition.

By his side stood a hairless dog, low on its legs, which was evidently barking at us. Yet we could hear nothing! The dog, it was plain, was dumb, and *barked at us in silence*!

Suddenly the man turned towards us, and said in a voice of the most exquisite politeness:

"Gentlemen, it is out of the question for you to return to La Chaux-de-Fonds tonight. Permit me to offer you my hospitality."

Then, bending over his dog, he said:

"Stop barking, Mystère."

The dog closed his jaws at once.

Makoko emitted a grunt. During the five hours that we had been enjoying the chase, Mathis and Makoko had told Allan and myself, who were strangers to the district, some strange and startling stories about our host, whom they represented as having had, like Faust, dealings with the Evil Spirit.

It was not without some trepidation, therefore, that we all moved out of the cavern.

"Gentlemen," said the stranger, with a melancholy smile, "it is many a long year since my door was thrown open to visitors. I am not fond of society, but I must tell you that one night, six months ago, a youth who had lost his way came and knocked at that door and begged for shelter till the morning. I refused him his request. Next day a body was found at the bottom of the big marl-pit – a body partly devoured by wolves."

"Why, that must have been Petit-Leduc!" cried Makoko. "So you were heartless enough to turn the poor lad away, at night and in the midst of winter! You are his murderer!"

"Truly spoken," replied the man, simply. "It was I who killed him. And now you see, gentlemen, that the incident has rendered me hospitable."

"Would you tell us why you drove him from your door?" growled Makoko.

"Because," he replied, quietly, "my house brings misfortune."

"I would rather risk meeting the powers of darkness than catching a cold in the head," I retorted, laughing, and without further parley we set off, and in a short while had reached the door of the ancient mansion, which stood among the most desolate surroundings, on a shelf of barren rock, swept by all the winds of heaven.

The huge door, antique, iron-barred, and studded with enormous nails, revolved slowly on its hinges, and opened noiselessly. A shrunken little old dame was there to welcome us.

From the threshold we could see a large, high room, somewhat similar to the room formerly styled the retainers' hall. It certainly constituted a part of what remained of the castle, on the ruins of which the mansion had been erected some centuries before. It was fully lighted by the fire on the enormous hearth, where a huge log was burning, and by two paraffin lamps hanging by chains from the stone roof. There was no furniture except a heavy table of white wood, a large armchair upholstered in leather, a few stools, and a rude sideboard.

We walked the length of the room. The old woman opened a door. We found ourselves at the foot of a worm-eaten staircase with sunken steps. This staircase, a spiral one, led to the second storey of the building, where the old woman showed us to our rooms.

To this day I can recall our host – were I to live a hundred years I could not forget that figure such as it appeared to me, as if framed by the fireplace – when I went into the hall where Mother Appenzel had spread our supper.

He was standing in front of my friends, on the stone hearth of that enormous fireplace. He was in evening dress – but such evening dress! It was in the pink of fashion, but a fashion long since vanished. The high collar of the coat, the broad lapels, the velvet waistcoat, the silken knee-breeches and stockings, the cravat, all seemed to possess the elegance of days gone by.

By his side lay his dog Mystère, his massive jaws parted in a yawn – yawning, just as he had barked, *in silence*.

"Has your dog been dumb for long?" I ventured to ask. "What strange accident has happened to him?"

"He has been dumb from his birth," replied my host, after a slight pause, as if this topic of conversation did not please him.

Still, I persisted in my questions.

"Was his father dumb – or perhaps his mother?"

"His mother, and his mother's mother," he replied, still coldly, "and *her* mother also."

"So you were the master of Mystère's great-grandmother?"

"I was, sir. She was indeed a faithful creature, and one who loved me well. A marvellous watchdog," added my host, displaying sudden signs of emotion which surprised me.

"And she also was dumb from her birth?"

"No, sir. No, she was not born dumb – *but she became so one night when she had barked too much!*"

There was a world of meaning in the tone with which he spoke these words that at the moment I did not understand.

Supper was served. During the meal the conversation did not languish. Our host inquired whether we liked our rooms.

"I have a favour to beg of you," I ventured to say. "I should like to sleep in the haunted room!"

No sooner had I uttered the sentence than our host's pale face became still paler.

"Who has told you that there was a haunted room in this house?" he asked, striving with difficulty to restrain an evident irritation.

Mother Appenzel, who had just entered, trembled violently.

"It was you, Mother Appenzel?"

"Pray do not scold the good woman," I said; "my indiscreet behaviour alone must bear the blame. I was attempting to enter a room the door of which was closed, when your servant forbade me to do so. 'Do not go into the haunted chamber,' she said."

"And you naturally did not do so?"

"Well, yes; I did go in."

"Heaven protect us!" wailed Mother Appenzel, letting fall a tumbler, which broke into pieces.

"Begone!" cried her master. Then, turning to us, he added, "You are indeed full of curiosity, gentlemen!"

"Pray pardon us if we are so," I said. "Moreover, permit me to remind you that it was you yourself who alluded to the rumours current on the mountain-side. Well, it would afford me much pleasure if your generous hospitality should be the occasion of dispersing them. When I have slept in the room which enjoys so evil a reputation, and have rested there peacefully, it will no longer be said that, to use your own expression, 'your house brings misfortune'."

Our host interrupted me: "You shall not sleep in that room; it is no longer used as a bedroom. No one has slept there for fifty years past."

"Who, then, was the last one to sleep in it?"

"I myself – and I should not advise anyone to sleep in it after me!"

"Fifty years ago, you say! You could only be a child at the time, at an age when one is still afraid at night – "

"Fifty years ago I was twenty-eight!"

"Am I committing an indiscretion when asking you what happened to you in that room? I have just come from visiting it, and nothing whatever happened to me. The room seems to me the most natural of rooms. I even attempted to prop up a wardrobe which seemed as if it were about to fall forwards on its face."

"You laid hands on the wardrobe!" cried the man, throwing down his table-napkin, and coming towards me with the gleam of madness in his eyes. "You actually laid hands on the wardrobe?"

"Yes," was my quiet answer; "as I say, it seemed about to fall."

"But it cannot fall! It will never fall! Never again will it stand upright! It is its nature to be in that position for all time to come, trembling with fear for all eternity!"

We had all risen. The man's voice was harsh as he spoke these most mysterious words. Heavy drops of perspiration trickled down his face. Those eyes of his, which we had thought dimmed for ever, flashed with fury. He was indeed awful to contemplate. He grasped my wrist and wrung it with a strength of which I would have deemed him incapable.

"You did not open it?"

"No."

"Then you do not know what is in it? No? Well, all the better! By Heaven, I tell you, sir, it is all the better for *you*!"

Turning towards his dog, he shouted:

"To your kennel! When will you find your voice again, Mystère? Or are you going to die like the others – *in silence*?"

He had opened the door leading to a tower, and went out, driving the dog before him.

We were deeply moved at this unexpected scene. The man had disappeared in the darkness of the tower, still pursuing his dog.

"What did I tell you?" remarked Makoko, in a scarcely

audible tone. "You may all please yourselves, but, as for me, I do not intend to sleep here tonight. I shall sit up here in this hall until daybreak."

"And so shall I," added Mathis.

Makoko, bending over us, his eyes staring out of their sockets, continued: "Do you not see that he is a madman?"

"You two fellows with your death-mask faces," exclaimed Allan, "are not going to prevent us from enjoying ourselves. Supposing we start a game of écarté. We will ask our host to take a hand; it will divert his thoughts."

An extraordinary fellow was Allan. His fondness for card-playing amounted to a mania. He pulled out a pack of cards, and had hardly done so when our host re-entered the hall. He was now comparatively calm, but no sooner had he perceived the pack of cards on the table than his features became transformed, and assumed such an expression of fear and fury that I myself was terrified.

"Cards!" he cried. "You have cards!"

Allan rose and said, pleasantly:

"We have decided not to retire for the night. We are about to have a friendly little game of écarté. Do you know the game?"

Allan stopped. He also had been struck with the fearful expression on our host's face. His eyes were bloodshot, the sparse hairs of his moustache stood out bristling, his teeth gleamed, while his lips hissed out the words:

"Cards! Cards!"

The words escaped with difficulty from his throat, as if some invisible hand were clutching it.

"Who sent you here with cards? What do you want with me? The cards must be burnt – they must be burnt!"

Of a sudden he grasped the pack and was about to cast it into the flames, but he stopped just on the point of doing so, his trembling fingers let drop the cards, and he sank into the arm-chair, exclaiming hoarsely:

"I am suffocating; I am suffocating!"

We rushed to his succour, but with a single effort of his bony fingers he had already torn off his collar and his cravat; and now, motionless, holding his head erect, and settling down in the huge armchair, he burst into tears.

"You are good fellows," he said at last, in milder tones. "You shall know everything. You shall not leave this house in ignorance, taking me for a madman – for a poor, miserable, melancholy madman.

"Yes, indeed," he continued; "yes, you shall know everything. It may be of use to you."

He rose, paced up and down, then halted in front of us, staring at us with the dimmed look that had given way to the momentary flash.

"Sixty years ago I was entering upon my eighteenth year. With all the overweening presumption of youth, I was sceptical of everything. Nature had fashioned me strong and handsome. Fate had endowed me with enormous wealth. I became the most fashionable youth of my day. Paris, gentlemen, with all its pleasures, was for ten years at my feet. When I had reached the age of twenty-eight I was on the brink of ruin. There remained to me between two and three hundred thousand francs and this manor, with the land surrounding it.

"Just at that time, gentlemen, I fell madly in love with an angelic creature. I could never have dreamt of the existence of such beauty and purity. The girl whom I adored was ignorant of the passionate love which was consuming me, and she remained so. Her family was one of the wealthiest in all Europe. For nothing in this world would I have had her suspect that I aspired to the honour of her hand in order to replenish my empty coffers with her dowry. So I went the way of the gambling-dens, in the vain hope of recovering my vanished millions. I lost all, and one fine evening I left Paris to come and bury myself in this old mansion, my sole refuge.

"I found here an old man, Father Appenzel; his granddaughter, of whom later on I made a servant; and his grandson, a child of tender years, who grew up to manhood on the estate, and who is now my steward. I fell a prey, on the very evening of my arrival, to despair and ennui. The astounding events that followed took place that very evening.

"When I went up to my room – the room which one of you has asked to be allowed to occupy tonight – I had made up my mind to take my own life. A brace of pistols lay on the chest of drawers. Suddenly, as I was putting my hand on one of the pistols, my dog began to howl in the courtyard – to howl as I have never heard the wind howl, unless it be tonight.

"So, thought I, here is Mystère raising a death-howl. She must know that I am going to kill myself tonight.

"I toyed with the pistol, recalling of a sudden what my past life had been, and wondering for the first time what my death would be like. Suddenly my eye lighted on the titles of a few old books which stood on a shelf hanging above the chest of drawers. I was surprised to see that all of them dealt with sorcerers and matters appertaining to the powers of evil. I took up a book, 'The Sorcerers of the Jura', and, with the sceptical smile of the man who had defied Fate, I opened it. The first two lines, printed in red, at once caught my eye:

" *'He who seriously wishes to see the devil has but to summon him with his whole heart, and he will come.'*

"Then followed the story of an individual who, like myself, a lover in despair – like myself, a ruined man – had in all sincerity summoned to his help the Prince of Darkness, and who had been assisted by him; for, a few months later, he had once more become incredibly rich and had married his beloved. I read the story to the end.

" 'Well, here was a lucky fellow!' I exclaimed, tossing the book on to the chest of drawers. Mystère was still howling in the grounds. I parted the window-curtains, and could not help shuddering when I saw the dog's shadow dancing in the moonlight. It really seemed as if the cur was possessed of some evil spirit, for her movements were inexplicably eccentric. She seemed to be snapping at some invisible form!

"I tried to laugh over the matter, but the state of my mind, the story I had just read, the howling of the dog, her strange leaps, the sinister locality, the old room, the pistols which I myself had loaded, all had contributed to take a greater hold of my imagination than I dared confess.

"Leaving the window I strolled about the room for a while. Of a sudden I saw myself in the mirror of the wardrobe. My pallor was such that I thought I was dead. Alas, No! The man standing before the wardrobe was not dead. It was, on the contrary, a living man who, with all his heart, was summoning the King of Lost Souls.

"Yes, with all my heart. I was too young to die; I wished to enjoy life for a while yet; to be rich once more; for her, for her sake, for the one who was an angel. Yes, yes, I, I myself summoned the devil!

"And then, in the mirror, side by side with my form, something appeared – something superhuman – a pale object – a mist, a terrible little cloud which was soon transformed into eyes – eyes of fearful loveliness. Another form was standing resplendent beside my haggard face; a mouth – a mouth which said to me, 'Open!' At this I recoiled. But the mouth was still saying to me, 'Open, open, if you dare!'

"Then something knocked three times upon the door inside the wardrobe – and the door flew open of its own accord!"

Just at that instant the old man's narrative was interrupted by three knocks on the door, which suddenly opened, and a man entered.

"Was it you who knocked like that, Guillaume?" asked our host, striving in vain to regain his composure.

"Yes, master."

"I had given you up for tonight. You saw the notary?"

"Yes; and I did not care to keep so great a sum of money about my person."

We gathered that Guillaume was the gentleman's steward. He advanced to the table, took a little bag from the folds of his cloak, extracted some documents from it, and laid them on the table. Then he drew an envelope from his bag, emptied its contents on the table, and counted out twelve one-thousand-franc notes.

"There's the purchase-money for Misery Wood."

"Good, Guillaume," said our host, picking up the bank-notes

and replacing them in the envelope. "You must be hungry. Are you going to sleep here tonight?"

"No; it is impossible. I have to call on the farmer. We have some business to transact together early in the morning. However, I do not mind having a bit of supper."

"Go to Mother Appenzel, my good fellow; she will take good care of you," adding, as the steward strode towards the kitchen, "Take away all those rubbishy papers."

The man picked up the documents, while the gentleman, taking a pocketbook out of his pocket, placed the envelope containing the twelve notes into it and returned the book to his pocket.

Then, resuming his narrative, in reply to a request from Makoko, he continued:

"You wish to know what the wardrobe contained? Well, I am going to tell you. There was something which I saw – something which scorched my eyes. There shone within the recess of the wardrobe, written in letters of fire, three words:

" 'THOU SHALT WIN!'

"Yes," he continued, in a gloomy tone, "the devil had, in three words, expressed in characters of fire, in the depths of the wardrobe, the fate that awaited me. He had left behind him his sign manual, the irrefutable proof of the hideous pact into which I had entered with him on that tragic night. 'Thou shalt win!' A ruined gamester, I sought to become rich, and he told me: 'Thou shalt win!' In three short words he granted me the world's wealth. 'Thou shalt win!'

"Next morning old Appenzel found me lying unconscious at the foot of the wardrobe. Alas! when I had recovered my senses I had forgotten nothing. I was fated never to forget what I had seen. Wherever I go, wherever I wend my steps, be it night, be it day, I read the fiery phrase, 'Thou shalt win!' – on the walls of darkness, on the resplendent orb of the sun, on the earth and in the skies, within myself when I close my eyes, on your faces when I look at you!"

The old man, exhausted, ceased speaking, and fell back, moaning, into the armchair.

"I must tell you," he resumed, after a few moments, "that my experience had had so terrifying an effect on me that I had been compelled to keep my bed, where Father Appenzel brought me a soothing potion of herbs. Addressing me, he said: 'Something incredible has happened, sir. Your dog has become dumb. *She barks in silence!*'

" 'Oh, I know, I understand!' I exclaimed. 'She will not recover her voice until *he* shall have returned!'

"Father Appenzel looked at me in amazement and fright, for my hair was standing on end. In spite of myself, my gaze was straying towards the wardrobe. Father Appenzel, as alarmed and agitated as myself, went on to say:

" 'When I found you, sir, on the floor this morning the wardrobe was inclined as it is now, while its door was open. I closed it, but I was unable to get it to stand upright. It seems always on the point of falling forwards.'

"I begged old Appenzel to leave me to myself. I got out of bed, went to the wardrobe, and opened its door. Conceive, I pray you, my feelings when I had done so. The sentence, that sentence written in characters of fire, was still there! It was graven in the boards at the back; it had burnt the boards with its imprint; and by day I read what I had read by night – the words: 'Thou shalt win.'

"I flew out of the room. I called for help. Father Appenzel returned. I said to him: 'Look into the depths of that wardrobe, and tell me what you see there!'

"My servant did as I bid him, and said to me: 'Thou shalt win!'

"I dressed myself. I fled like a madman from the accursed house, and wandered in the mountains. The mountain air did me good. When I came home in the evening I was perfectly calm; I had thought matters over; my dog might have become dumb through some perfectly natural physiological phenomenon. With regard to the sentence in the wardrobe, it had not come there of itself, and, as I had not had any previous acquaintance with that piece of furniture, it was probable that the three fatal words had been there for countless years, inscribed by someone addicted to the black art, following upon some gambling affair which was no concern of mine.

"I ate my supper, and went to bed in the same room. The night passed without incident.

"Next day I went to La Chaux-de-Fonds, to call on a notary. All that this adventure with the wardrobe had succeeded in doing was to imbue me with the idea of tempting fate, in the shape of cards, one last time, before putting into execution my idea about suicide. I borrowed a few one-thousand-franc notes on the security of the estate, and I took the train for Paris. As I ascended the staircase of the club I recalled my nightmare, and remarked to myself ironically, for I placed no faith in the success of this supreme attempt: 'We shall now see whether, if the devil helps me – ' I did not finish the sentence.

"The bank was being put up to auction when I entered the salon. I secured it for two hundred louis. I had not reached the middle of my deal when I had already won two hundred and fifty thousand francs! But no longer would any of the players stake against me. *I was winning every game!*

"I was jubilant; I had never dreamt that such luck would be mine. I threw up the bank – i.e., what remained of it for me to hold. I next amused myself at throwing away chances, just to see what would happen. In spite of this I continued winning. Exclamations were heard on all sides. The players vowed I had the devil's own luck. I collected my winnings and left.

"No sooner had I reached the street than I began to think and to become alarmed. The coincidence between the scene of the wardrobe and of my extraordinary success as a banker troubled me. Of a sudden, and to my surprise, I found myself wending my way back to the club. I was resolved to probe the matter to the bottom. My shortlived joy was disturbed by the fact that I had not lost once. So it was that I was anxious to lose just once.

"When I left the club for the second time, at six o'clock in the morning, I had won, in money and promises, no less than a couple of millions. But I had not once lost – not a single, solitary time. I felt myself becoming a raving madman. When I say that I had not lost once, I speak with regard to money, for when I had played for nothing, without stakes, to see, just for the fun of the matter, I lost inexorably. But no sooner had a punter staked even as low as half a franc against me, I won his money. It mattered little, a sou or a million francs. I could no longer lose. 'Thou shalt win!' Oh, that terrible curse! That curse! For a whole week did I try. I went into the worst gambling-hells. I sat down to card-tables presided over by card-sharpers; I won even from them; I won from one and all against whom I played. I did nothing but win!

"So, you no longer laugh, gentlemen! You scoff no more! You see now, good sirs, that one should never be in a hurry to laugh! I told you I had seen the devil! Do you believe me now? I possessed then the certainty, the palpable proof, visible to one and all, the natural and terrestrial proof of my revolting compact with the devil. The law of probabilities no longer existed as far as I was concerned. There were not even any probabilities. There remained only the supernatural certainty of winning eternally – until the day of death. Death! I could no longer dream of it as a desire. For the first time in my life I dreaded it. The terrors of death haunted me, because of what awaited me at the end!

"My uppermost thought was to redeem my soul – my wretched, my lost soul. I frequented the churches. I saw priests. I prostrated myself at the foot of church steps. I beat my delirious head on the sacred flagstones! I prayed to God that I might lose, just as I had prayed to the devil that I might win. On leaving the holy place I was wont to hurry to some low gambling-den and stake a few louis on a card. But I continued winning for ever and ever! 'Thou shalt win!'

"Not for a single second did I entertain the idea of owing my happiness to those accursed millions. I offered up my heart to God as a burnt-offering, I distributed the millions I had won to the poor, and I came here, gentlemen, to await the death which spurns me – the death I dread!"

"You have never played since those days?" I asked.

"I have never played from that time until now."

Allan had read my thoughts. He too was dreaming that it might be possible to rescue from his monomania the man whom we both persisted in considering insane.

"I feel sure," he said, "that so great a sacrifice has won you pardon. Your despair has been undoubtedly sincere, and your punishment a terrible one. What more could Heaven require of you? In your place, *I should try* – "

"You would try – what?" exclaimed the man, springing from his seat.

"I should try whether I were still doomed to win!"

The man struck the table a violent blow with his clenched fist.

"And so this is all the remedy you can suggest! So this is all the narrative of a curse transcending all things earthly has inspired you with? You seek to induce an old lunatic to play, with the object of demonstrating to him that he is not insane! For I read full well in your eyes what you think of me: 'He is mad, mad, mad!' You do not believe a single word of all I have told you. You think I am insane, young man! And you, too," he added, addressing Allan, "you think I am insane – mad, mad, mad! I tell you that I have seen the devil! Yes, your old madman has seen the devil! And he is going to prove it to you. The cards! Where are the cards?"

Espying them on the edge of the table, he sprang on them.

"It is you who have so willed it. I had harboured a supreme hope that I should die without having again made the infernal attempt, so that when my hour had come I might imagine that Heaven had forgiven me. Here are your cards! I will not touch them. They are yours. Shuffle them – deal me which you please – 'stack' them as you will. I tell you that I shall win. Do you believe me now?"

Allan had quietly picked up the cards.

The man, placing his hand on his shoulder, asked, "You do not believe me?"

"We shall see," replied Allan.

"What shall the stakes be?" I inquired.

"I do not know, gentlemen, whether you are well off or not, but I feel bound to inform you – you who have come to destroy my last hope – that you are ruined men."

Thereupon he took out his pocketbook and laid it on the table, saying:

"I will play you five straight points at écarté for the contents of this pocketbook. This just by way of a beginning. After that, I am willing to play you as many games as you see fit, until I cast you out of doors picked clean, your friends and yourself, ruined for the rest of your lives – yes, picked bare."

"Picked bare?" repeated Allan, who was far less moved than myself. "Do you want even our shirts?"

"Even your souls," cried the man, "which I intend to present to the devil in exchange for my own."

Allan winked at me, and asked:

"Shall we say 'Done', and go halves in this?"

I agreed, shuffled the pack, and handed it to my opponent.

He cut. I dealt. I turned up the knave of hearts. Our host looked at his hand and led. Clearly he ought not to have played the hand he held – three small clubs, the queen of diamonds, and the seven of spades. He took a trick with his queen. I took the four others, and, as he had led, I marked two points. I entertained not the slightest doubt that he was doing his utmost to lose.

It was his turn to deal. He turned up the king of spades. He could not restrain a shudder when he beheld that black faced card, which, in spite of himself, gave him a trick.

He scanned his hand anxiously. It was my turn to call for cards. He refused them, evidently believing that he held a very poor hand: but my own was as bad as his, and he had a ten of hearts, which took my nine – I held the nine, eight, and seven of hearts.

He then played diamonds, to which I could not respond, and two clubs higher than mine. Neither of us held a single trump. He scored a point, which, with the one secured to him by his king, gave him two. We were "evens", either of us being in a position to end matters at once if we made three points.

The deal was mine. I turned up the eight of diamonds. This time both of us called for cards. He asked for one, and showed me the one he had discarded – the seven of diamonds. He was anxious not to hold any trumps. His wish was gratified, and he succeeded in making me score another two points, which gave me four.

In spite of ourselves, Allan and I glanced towards the

pocketbook. Our thoughts ran: "There lies a small fortune which is shortly to be ours, one which, in all conscience, we shall not have had much trouble in winning."

Our host dealt in his turn, and when I saw the cards he had given me I considered the matter as good as settled. This time he had not turned up a king, but the seven of clubs. I held two hearts and three trumps – the ace and king of hearts, the ace, ten, and nine of clubs. I led the king, my opponent followed with the queen; I flung the ace on the table, my opponent being compelled to take it with a knave of hearts, and he then played a diamond, which I trumped. I played the ace of trumps; he took it with the queen, but I was ready for him with my last card, the ten of clubs. He had the knave of trumps! As I had led he scored two, making "four all". Our host smothered a curse which was hovering on his lips.

"No need for you to worry," I remarked; "no one has won yet."

"We are about to prove to you," said Allan, in the midst of a deathly silence, "that you can lose just like any ordinary mortal."

Our host groaned, "I cannot lose."

The interest in the game was now at its height. A point on either side, and either of us would be the winner. If I turned up the king the game was ended, and I won twelve thousand francs from a man who claimed that he could not lose. I had death. I turned up the king – the king of hearts. I had won!

My opponent uttered a cry of joy. He bent over the card, picked it up, considered it attentively, fingered it, raised it to his eyes, and we thought he was about to press it to his lips. He murmured:

"Great heavens, can it be? Then – then I have lost!"

"So it would seem," I remarked.

Allan added, "You now see full well that one should not place any faith in what the devil says."

The gentleman took his pocketbook and opened it.

"Gentlemen," he sighed, "bless you for having won all that is in this book. Would that it contained a million! I should gladly have handed it over to you."

With trembling hands he searched the pocketbook, emptying it of all its contents, with a look of surprise at not finding at once the twelve thousand francs he had deposited in its folds. They were not there!

The pocketbook, searched with feverish hands, lay empty on the table. *There was nothing in the pocketbook! Nothing!*

We sat dumbfounded at this inexplicable phenomenon – the empty pocketbook. We picked it up and fingered it. We searched it carefully, only to find it empty! Our host, livid and as one possessed, was searching himself and begging us to search him. We searched him – we searched him, because it was beyond our power to resist his delirious will; but we found nothing – nothing!

"Hark!" exclaimed our host. "Hark, hark! Does it not seem to you tonight that the wind sounds like the voice of a dog?"

We listened, and Makoko answered, "It is true! The wind really seems to be barking – there, behind the door!"

The door was shaking strangely, and we heard a voice calling, "Open!"

I drew the bolts and opened the door. A human form rushed into the room.

"It is the steward," I said.

"Sir, sir!" he ejaculated.

"What is it?" we all exclaimed, breathlessly, and wondering what was about to follow.

"Sir, I thought I had handed you your twelve thousand francs. Indeed, I am positive I did so. Those gentlemen doubtless saw me."

"Yes, indeed," from all of us.

"Well, I have just discovered them in my bag. I cannot understand how it has happened. I have returned to bring them back to you – *once more*. Here they are."

The steward again pulled out the identical envelope, and a second time counted the twelve one-thousand-franc notes, adding:

"I know now what ails the mountainside tonight, but it terrifies me. I shall sleep here."

The twelve thousand francs were now lying on the table. Our host cried:

"This time we see them, there before us! Where are the cards? Deal them. The twelve thousand in five straight points, to see, to know for certain. I tell you that I wish to know – *to know*."

I dealt. My opponent called for cards: I refused them. He had five trumps. He scored two points. He dealt the cards. He turned up the king. I led. He again had five trumps. Three and two are five! He had won!

Then he howled: yes, howled like the wind which had the voice of a dog. He snatched the cards from the table and cast them into the flames. "Into the fire with the cards! Let the fire consume them!" he shrieked.

Suddenly he strode towards the door. Outside a dog barked – a dog raising a death howl.

The man reached the door, and speaking through it asked:

"Is that you, Mystère?"

To what phenomenon was it due that both wind and dog were silent simultaneously?

The man softly drew the bolts and half opened the door. No sooner was the door ajar than the infernal yelping broke out so prolonged and so lugubrious that it made us shiver to our very marrow. Our host had now flung himself upon the door with such force that we could almost think he had smashed it. Not content with having pushed back the bolts, he pressed with his knees and arms against the door, without uttering a sound. All we heard was his panting respiration.

Then, when the death-like yelping had ceased, and both within and without silence reigned supreme, the man, turning towards us and tottering forward, said:

"He has returned! Beware!"

Midnight. We have gone our respective ways. Makoko and Mathis have remained below beside the dying embers. Allan has sought his bedroom, while, driven by some unknown inner force controlling me absolutely, I find myself in the haunted

room. I am repeating the doings of the man whose story we had
heard that night: I select the same book, open it at the same
page; I go to the same window; I pull the curtain aside; I gaze
upon the same moonlit landscape, for the wind has long since
driven off the tempest-clouds and the fog. I only see bare rocks,
shining like steel under the rays of the bright moon, and – on
the desolate plateau – a weirdly dancing shadow – the shadow
of Mystère, with her formidable jaws wide apart – jaws that I
can see barking. Do I hear the barking? Yes; it seems to me that
I hear it. I let the curtain drop. I take my candlestick from the
chest of drawers. I step towards the wardrobe. I look at myself
in its mirrored panel. I dream of *him* who wrote the words
which lie concealed within. Whose face is it that I see in the
mirror? It is my own! But is it possible that the face of our
host on the fatal night could have been more pallid than mine is
now? In all truth, my face is that of a dead man. On one side –
there – there – that little cloud – that misty cloudlet in the
mirror – cheek by jowl with my face – those fearful eyes – those
lips! Oh, if I could but scream! I cannot. I am powerless to cry
out, *when suddenly I hear three knocks.* And – and my hand
strays of its own accord towards the door of the wardrobe – my
inquisitive hand – my accursed hand.

Of a sudden my hand is gripped in the vice I know so well. I
look round. I am face to face with our host, who says to me in a
voice which seems to come from another world:

"*Do not open it!*"

Epilogue

Next morning we did not ask our host to give us the opportunity of winning back our money. We fled from his roof without
even taking leave of him. Twelve thousand francs were sent that
evening to our strange host through Makoko's father, to whom
we had told our adventure. He returned them to us, with the
following note:

"We are quits. When we played, both the first game, which
you won, and the second one, which you lost, we *believed,* you
and I, that we were staking twelve thousand francs. That must be

sufficient for us. The devil has my soul, but he shall not possess my honour."

We were not at all anxious to keep the twelve thousand francs, so we presented them to a hospital in La Chaux-de-Fonds which was in sore need of money. Following upon urgent repairs, to which our donation was applied, the hospital, one winter's night, was so thoroughly burned to the ground that at noon of the following day nothing but ashes remained of it.

THE GOLD AXE

MANY YEARS AGO I was at Gersau, a small health resort on the Lake of the Four Forest Cantons, a few miles from Lucerne. I wanted to complete certain work, and I had arranged to spend the autumn in the quiet of this delightful village whose ancient pointed roofs were reflected in the romantic waters of the lake on which William Tell sailed in days of old.

It was the end of autumn, and tourists had scattered, while the many hideous Tartars who had descended upon us from Germany with their alpenstocks, their puttees and their little round hats decked with the indispensable feather, had returned to their lager, their sauerkraut and their "big concerts", leaving the country between Pilatus, the Mythen and the Rigi free to us at last.

Not more than half a dozen of us foregathered in the hotel at meal time, and when evening came related our experiences of the day or indulged in a little music.

An old lady, always enveloped in deep mourning, who when the little hotel was swarming with noisy visitors had never addressed a word to anyone, and seemed the embodiment of woe, stood revealed as a pianist of the first rank, and without waiting to be pressed, played Chopin to us and, in particular, a certain lullaby by Schumann which she rendered with such exquisite tenderness that she brought tears to our eyes.

We were all so grateful to her for the pleasant hours which she enabled us to pass, that we joined together to present her at the moment of her departure, with a slight souvenir of our stay at Gersau.

One of us who went that day to Lucerne undertook to buy the gift. He returned in the evening with a gold brooch in the form of a small axe.

Neither on that evening nor the following one did the old lady make her appearance; and the visitors who were leaving entrusted the gold brooch to my care.

Her luggage was still in the hotel, and I was prepared to see her return, sooner or later, reassured as to her wellbeing by the proprietor who told me that she was in the habit of disappearing for a day or two, and he had no reason to feel anxious about her.

As a matter of fact the day before my departure, as I was making a final tour of the lake and had pulled up a few steps from Tell's Chapel, I saw the old lady standing at the entrance of the building.

Never until then had I been impressed by the unspeakable distress depicted on her face down which the tears were coursing, and never had I so clearly observed the traces, which were still manifest, of her former beauty. She caught sight of me, lowered her veil, and walked towards the lake. Nevertheless I did not hesitate to overtake her, and bowing, expressed the visitors' regret that we were about to lose her; and then, as I had the gift on me, I presented her with the small case containing the gold axe.

She opened it with a sweet, faraway smile, but no sooner did she perceive the jewel inside than she began to tremble with emotion, and drew back some distance from me, as though she had something to fear from my presence, and with an insensate gesture threw the brooch into the lake.

I displayed so much amazement at this unaccountable reception that she begged my forgiveness and burst into a fit of sobbing. A seat stood in this secluded spot, and we both sat down. And after a few lamentations against the decrees of fate which left me quite at a loss, she confided to me her strange, melancholy story which I was never to forget. For, in truth, I know of no more terrible destiny than that which befell the old lady in the black veil, who had played Schumann's lullaby to us with such exquisite emotion.

"I will tell you the whole story," she said, "for I am about to leave forever this country which I determined to visit for the last time.

And then you will understand why it was that I threw the little gold axe into the lake.

"I was born in Geneva, monsieur. We belonged to one of the leading families and were rich, but some unfortunate speculations on the stock exchange ruined my father, who died from the shock. When I was eighteen I was a beautiful girl without a dowry. My mother gave up all hope of marrying me. And yet she yearned to make sure of my future before she went to join my father.

"I was twenty-four when a suitor whom everyone looked upon as an unhoped-for chance appeared.

"A young man from Briesgau who was accustomed to spend the summer in Switzerland and whose acquaintance we made in the casino at Evian, fell in love with me, and I liked him. Herbert Gutmann was a tall young fellow, kindly, unobtrusive and good-natured. He seemed to unite qualities alike of heart and mind. He possessed a certain affluence without being actually wealthy. His father was still engaged in business, and made him an allowance in order that he might travel until the time came for him to succeed him in his business. We were all intending to visit the elder Gutmann at his place in Todtnau, in the Black Forest, when the state of my mother's health greatly hastened the course of events.

"Conscious that she no longer possessed the physical strength to travel, my mother hurriedly returned to Geneva, where she received from the civil authorities of Todtnau, to whom she had written, the most satisfactory information in respect of Herbert and his family. Herbert's father had begun life as an ordinary woodcutter, and then had left the district, returning to it with a small fortune which he had 'made in timber'. That was all, at least, that was known of him in Todtnau.

"This was enough to induce my mother to press forward the formalities of my marriage, which took place a week before her death. She died with her mind at rest for, as she said, she felt 'reassured about my future'.

"My husband helped me to overcome the grief which this sore trial caused me by his constant goodness and solicitude. Before we set out for Todtnau we came here to Gersau to spend a week, and then to my great surprise we undertook a long journey instead of making our visit to Herbert's father. My sorrow would have gradually been dispelled if, as the days sped by, I had not noticed, almost with dismay, that my husband was more and more becoming a prey to melancholy.

"I was more surprised than I can express, because Herbert had seemed to me of a humorous disposition, open, unrestrained and extremely frank. Was I to discover that the liveliness which he used to display was forced, and veiled some deep mortification? Alas! his sighs when he thought himself alone, and the agitation which sometimes disturbed his night's rest, scarcely left room for doubt, and I made up my mind to question him.

"At the first word that I ventured to speak on the subject he made answer by bursting into laughter, treating me as a silly little goose and kissing me passionately, which merely served to strengthen my conviction that I was in the presence of some painful mystery.

"I could not hide from myself that there was something in Herbert's demeanour which was very like 'remorse'. And yet I could have sworn that he was incapable of committing, I will not say a low or mean action, but even one lacking in propriety.

"It was then that the fate which had dogged my footsteps struck us another blow in the person of my father-in-law, of whose death we learnt whilst we were in Scotland. This grievous piece of news depressed my husband more than I can say. He remained the whole night without uttering a word, nor did he shed tears nor appear to listen to the words of consolation by which I, in my turn, endeavoured to rouse his spirit. He seemed to be overwhelmed. At last, when the light was beginning to dawn, he rose from the armchair in which he had sat huddled, and turning towards me a face terribly distorted by suffering, said in a harrowing voice:

" 'Come, Elizabeth, we shall have to go back. We shall have to go back.'

"These words seemed to possess a significance from the tone in which they were spoken which I failed to understand. A return to the land of his fathers was quite natural at a moment like that; I could not see why he should fight against the necessity of going home. From that day onward Herbert changed completely; he grew extraordinarily silent, and more than once I came upon him sobbing wildly.

"The grief which the loss of a beloved father might occasion could not entirely explain the horror of our position, for there is nothing more terrible than mystery, the deep mystery which steals in between two beings who are devoted to each other, and separates them from their happiness . . .

"We reached Todtnau in time to breathe a prayer over the newly-made grave.

"This little town in the Black Forest, at no great distance from Höllenthal, was a dreary spot; and there was scarcely any society in it for me. The Gutmanns' house, in which we took up our abode, lay on the borders of the forest.

"It was a gloomy chalet standing in its own grounds, and our one visitor was an old clockmaker in the place, who was said to be rich and had been the elder Gutmann's friend. He appeared from time to time at the lunch or dinner hour, in order to get himself invited.

"I had no liking for this manufacturer of cuckoo clocks, this petty usurer, for though he was rich, he was a miser and incapable of the least nicety of feeling. Nor did Herbert care for Franz Basckler, though he continued out of respect for the memory of his father to keep on friendly terms with him.

"Basckler, who had no children, had told the elder Gutmann times out of number that Herbert was his only heir. Herbert spoke to me about it one day with the most sincere aversion, and I had once more an opportunity of appreciating the strictness of his conscience.

" 'Would you like to be the heir of this sordid old miser who made his fortune by ruining all the clockmakers in Höllenthal?'

" 'Certainly not,' I returned. 'Your father left us a certain amount of property and with what you can honestly earn we shall have enough to live on even if Heaven chooses to send us a child.'

"I had no sooner uttered these words than I saw my Herbert

turn as white as a sheet. I put my arms round him, for I thought
that he was about to faint, but the blood returned to his face, and
he exclaimed in forcible tones:

"'Yes, yes, the only true thing is to have the approbation of
one's conscience.'

"And so saying he rushed wildly from the room.

"Sometimes he was away for a day or two on business, which
consisted, he told me, of buying plantations of standing trees and
selling them again to contractors. He did not work the whole
thing himself but left to others the task of turning the trees into
sleepers for railways, if the wood was of inferior quality, and
posts and ships' masts if it was of the best quality. The essential
thing was to display expert judgment; and he had acquired his
knowledge of timber from his father.

"He never took me away with him on any of his journeys. He
left me alone in the house with an old maidservant who had
received me with ill-disguised hostility. I kept out of her way and
wept in secret, for I was not happy. I felt convinced that Herbert
was hiding something from me, something which was obsessing
his mind, and which I too, who knew nothing, was never able to
dismiss from my thoughts.

"And then the great forest frightened me. And the servant
frightened me. And old Basckler frightened me. And the old
house! It was very large with staircases everywhere leading to
passages into which I dared not venture. At the end of one of
them in particular, stood a small room. I had seen my husband
enter it two or three times, but I myself had never set foot in it.

"I could not pass the door of this room, which was always
closed, without a tremor. It was to this study that Herbert was
wont to retire, so he told me, to make up his accounts and
balance his books, but it was also to this room that he retired
alone to bewail his secret.

"One night after he had set out on one of his journeys and I
was vainly endeavouring to sleep, my attention was attracted by
a slight sound under my window which I had left partly open on
account of the extreme heat. I got out of bed with every
precaution. The sky was overcast and great clouds hid the stars

from sight. It was as much as I could do to discern the threatening shadows of the nearest trees which faced the house.

"I could not clearly distinguish my husband and the maidservant until they passed under my window, walking on the lawn with infinite caution so that I should not hear the sound of their footsteps and carrying between them a sort of long, somewhat narrow trunk which I had never before seen. They entered the chalet and I did not hear nor see them again for the next ten minutes.

"My anguish exceeded anything that it is possible to conceive. Why were they hiding themselves from me? How was it that I had not heard the coming of the chaise which usually brought Herbert home? Just then I seemed to catch in the distance the neighing of a horse, and the maidservant appeared, crossed the lawn, vanished in the darkness, and soon returned leading our mare unharnessed over the soft ground. Never had they taken so many precautions to prevent me from waking up!

"Growing more and more surprised that Herbert did not come to our room as was his custom after his return at night, I hastily slipped on a dressing gown and wandered into the darkness of the passage. My steps turned quite naturally towards the little study of which I stood in so much fear. And I had only just entered the corridor which led to it when I heard my husband say in a rough, muffled voice to the maidservant who was mounting the stairs:

" 'Water! Bring me some water. Hot water of course. It won't come off.'

"I stopped short and held my breath. Besides I could not breathe. I was stifling. I was filled with the presentiment that some dreadful misfortune had befallen us. Suddenly I was once more startled by my husband's voice:

" 'Ah at last! That's done it. It's come off.'

"My husband and the old woman were still talking in low tones and I heard his step. That brought me to myself and I fled to my bedroom and locked myself in. Soon he knocked at the door and I went through the form of pretending to be asleep and to wake up, and at last I opened the door. I held a candle in my hand which fell to the floor when I caught sight of the look on his face.

" 'What's the matter?' he asked. 'Are you still asleep? Do go back to bed.'

"I made a movement to light the candle again, but he stopped me and I threw myself on the bed. I spent a cruel night.

"Herbert turned and tossed and sighed beside me and could not sleep. He did not speak a word. At daybreak he rose, pressed an icy kiss on my brow and left the room. When I got downstairs the old woman gave me a note from him in which he stated that he was obliged to go away again for a couple of days.

"At eight o'clock that morning I learned from workmen on their way to Neustadt, that old Basckler had been found murdered in a small cottage which he possessed at Höllenthal, where he sometimes spent the night when his business of moneylending kept him too long among his peasant-debtors. Basckler had received a terrible blow with an axe which had split his head in two. It was undoubtedly the work of a woodman.

"I returned to the house as best I could. Once again I tried to enter that little study, but I was frustrated by the old servant. "Leave that room alone. You know M. Gutmann has forbidden you to touch it,' she said.

"I took to my bed, suffering from a high fever, and was ill for a fortnight. Herbert looked after me with solicitude, and when I recovered it first seemed that I had been the sport of some evil dream. Moreover, the murderer of Basckler had been arrested. He was a woodman named Mathis Müller of Bergen whom, it was said, the old miser had 'bled', and who had taken his revenge by 'bleeding' his persecutor, although he protested his innocence.

"Our circumstances were in no way affected, as we imagined they might be, by old Basckler's death, and Herbert looked in vain for a will which did not exist. Its absence considerably upset him and a black look came over his face whenever it was mentioned.

"During Mathis Müller's trial at Freiburg I eagerly read the newspapers; and certain words which fell from the counsel for the defence haunted me day and night:

" 'Until you have discovered the axe with which the deed was done and the murderer's bloodstained clothes, you cannot convict Mathis Müller.'

"Nevertheless Mathis Müller was found guilty and sentenced to death, and I am bound to say that the verdict strangely affected my husband. At night he dreamed of nothing but Mathis Müller. I was terrified of him and my thoughts also terrified me.

"Oh I longed to know the truth! I was determined to know the truth. What was the meaning of those words: 'It won't come off?'

"What was the nature of the work upon which he was engaged in the mysterious little study during the night?

"One night I rose and groping in the dark stole his keys from him. I crept into the corridors. I went to the kitchen to fetch a lantern. With chattering teeth I reached the forbidden room . . . I opened the door and my eyes at once fell on the trunk – the oblong trunk which had so greatly perplexed me.

"It was locked, but I had no difficulty in finding the small key on the bunch . . . I unlocked it and raised the lid. I went down on my knees in order to see better, and the sight that met my eyes forced a cry of horror from me . . .

"The trunk contained bloodstained clothes and the axe which had struck the blow still spotted with rust . . .

"How I managed, after what I had seen, to live with Herbert through the few weeks which preceded the convicted man's execution I cannot tell . . .

"I was afraid that he might kill me . . .

"How was it that my attitude, the dread that possessed me, failed to enlighten him? The fact is that at that time his mind was wholly a prey to fears not less great than my own. The thought of Mathis Müller never left him.

"To enable him to escape the obsession, apparently, he now shut himself up in the little study, and I sometimes heard him delivering tremendous blows, which made the floor and walls resound, as if he were fighting with his axe against the ghosts and phantoms which beset him.

"Strange to say, and it seemed at first impossible to understand, Herbert recovered his calmness a couple of days before

Müller's execution – the calmness of marble, the calmness of a statue. That evening he said:

" 'I am going away tomorrow morning early. I have some important business to do near Freiburg. I shall probably be away for a couple of days. Don't worry.'

"It was at Freiburg that the execution was to take place, and I had the impression that Herbert's composure was the result of the resolution that he had taken.

"He was going to give himself up!

"The thought was so much of a relief to me that for the first time for many a night I fell into a sound sleep. It was broad daylight when I awoke. My husband had already left the house.

"I dressed in haste and without saying a word to the old servant I started for Todtnau. Here, I took a conveyance and drove to Freiburg. I reached Freiburg when the light had begun to wane. I went at once to the Court House, and the first person whom I saw entering the building was my husband. I stood rooted to the spot. And as Herbert did not come out again I felt sure that he had surrendered and was being held there at the disposal of the authorities.

"The prison at that time was next to the Court House. I walked round it like a madwoman. All that night I wandered about the streets, returning every now and then to this gloomy building, and the first gleams of day were beginning to break when my eyes encountered two men clad in black frockcoats mounting the front steps of the Court.

"I ran up to them and said that I wanted to see the public prosecutor as soon as possible as I had a communication of the utmost gravity to make to him about the Basckler murder.

"As it happened, one of the gentlemen was the public prosecutor, and he invited me to accompany him to his office. Here I explained who I was and said that he must have received a visit from my husband the night before. He told me that he had in fact seen him, and then as he took refuge in silence I threw myself on my knees before him beseeching him to have pity on me and tell me whether Herbert had confessed his crime. He seemed surprised, helped me to rise to my feet, and questioned me.

"Slowly I told him the story of my life, such as I have told it to you, and at last I described the awful discovery which I had made in the little study in the chalet at Todtnau. I ended by declaring that I should never have allowed an innocent man to be executed, and that had not my husband given himself up, I should not have hesitated to inform the police. And then I asked him as a final act of mercy, to be allowed to see Herbert.

" 'Yes, you shall see him, madame,' he said. 'Come with me.'

"He took me, more dead than alive, to the prison, through the corridors and up a staircase. Here he stood me before a small barred window which jutted over a large hall and left me, telling me to have patience. A number of other persons soon took up their positions at this window, and looked into the hall.

"I did as they did. It was as though I was fastened to the bars, and I had the feeling that I was about to witness some monstrous spectacle.

"The hall was gradually lined with a number of persons all of whom maintained a mournful silence. Daylight now rendered the scene more visible. In the centre of the hall we could clearly discern a heavy block of wood, and someone exclaimed:

" 'That's the headsman's block!'

"So Müller was to be executed! An icy perspiration began to trickle down my forehead, and I cannot say even now how it was that I did not fall into a dead faint. A door opened, and a procession appeared headed by the condemned man, quivering in his shirt which was cut low and showed his bare neck. His hands were bound behind his back, and he was supported by two warders. A minister of religion was murmuring in his ear.

"The wretched man began to speak. In a few trembling words he confessed his crime and asked forgiveness of God and man. A civic officer took note of the confession and read out the sentence of the Court; and then the two warders thrust the convict on his knees and placed his head on the block.

"Mathis Müller might have already been dead for all the sign of life he gave, when a man with bare arms, carrying an axe on his shoulder, stepped forward from the side where he had hitherto remained in the background.

"This man placed his hand upon the prisoner's head, waved the two warders aside, lifted the axe and struck a terrible blow. Nevertheless he had to strike a second time before the head fell. Then he picked it up by the hair and stood erect.

"How was it that I was able to watch the unspeakably horrible sight until the end? Yet I could not remove my eyes from this scene of blood, and it seemed as though there was still something for me to see, and indeed my eyes did see . . . they saw, when holding his shaking hand the abominable trophy, the executioner drew himself up and raised his eyes.

"I uttered a piercing shriek, 'Herbert!' and fell unconscious."

"Now, monsieur, you know my story. I had married the public executioner. The axe which I had discovered in the little study was the executioner's axe; the bloodstained clothes were the executioner's clothes.

"Next day I fled to the house of an old relative, and I very nearly lost my reason; and I don't know how it is that I am still in this world.

"As for my husband who could not live without me, for he loved me more than anything on earth, he was found two months later hanging in our room. I received a last letter from him:

" 'Forgive me, Elizabeth, I have tried every sort of occupation. I was dismissed as soon as it was discovered that I was the son of my father. I was forced at an early age to make up my mind to take up the succession of his work. You will understand now how it is that the office of public executioner descends from father to son. I was born an honest man, and the only crime that I have committed was to conceal the truth from you . . . Farewell!' "

While I stood gazing in dumb amazement at the spot in the lake where the lady in black had thrown the little gold axe, she disappeared in the distance.

THE WAXWORK MUSEUM

ONE WINTER'S EVENING four young men were dining in a fashionable French restaurant on one of the boulevards. The room was brilliantly lit with great silver lamps, the reflection from which caught the women's jewels making them flash like fire. The Hungarian band played soft, sentimental waltzes.

It was that time of the day which lends itself to romance. The storm outside accentuated the warmth and comfort of the room. Man is an egoist, and it is only when he pauses to compare his mode of living with that of those who are less fortunate than himself that he fully appreciates his luck. Whilst the quartette sat over their wine their thoughts strayed to the slums where, at that moment, "down and outs", soaked through to the skin and buffeted by the wind, would be dragging in the streets seeking in vain for shelter. Being extremely young they revelled in this conversation, conjuring up vivid pictures and sparing no detail.

The eldest of the four was a good-looking fair-haired boy named Pierre de Lienne. "It is an ideal night to plan a crime," he remarked laughingly, tilting his chair and blowing smoke rings towards the ceiling.

"When authors invent a murder story they never fail to call the elements to their aid. For example," he continued, "imagine the stage in a theatre with sinister scenery. It is wet and stormy, and one of the unfortunate men, of whom we have been talking, enters. In a crevice of the wall one can see the murderer hiding, a knife gleaming in his hand! Imagine the tension in the audience! The effect is instantaneous."

He broke off, pointing to one of his companions. "Why, look at Jacques, he's scared already!" he exclaimed.

"Yes, you are quite right," replied the boy, who had been listening with rapt attention. "I hate these gruesome stories.

Can't we talk about something else?" he asked, pouring out some wine.

They all laughed.

"I have always been nervous," said Jacques. "As a small child I was terrified of going upstairs alone after dark, but my people made me do it. I used to scream and yell, clinging to the banisters and refusing to move. This fear was due to the fantastic stories I had heard from my nurse about blood-curdling inns on the side of lonely roads, where they roasted strangers in the oven; of highwaymen who, in plundering, forced their victims to undergo the most frightful tortures; of nightly apparitions; women clothed in white; corpses awoken from eternal sleep and ghosts fettered with chains. She wrecked my nerves, the stupid woman. Of course, I am braver now, though I still look under my bed before going to sleep!"

"But the very fact that you have the courage to look shows that you aren't really frightened," said his neighbour, Louis Monnier. "What would you do if you found a man hidden there?"

"Oh! well," replied Jacques, "I suppose I realise that my fears are purely imaginative. It is a case of laying the ghost."

"Fear comes from within," said Pierre. "It is unaccountable and cannot be explained. Often there seems no cause for it, and with many it is a nervous illness. The man who is healthy in mind and body knows no fear, but with highly-strung people it is an incurable malady."

"Here, steady," interrupted Jacques. "I am as healthy in body and mind as you are."

"A moment ago you said you had disordered nerves."

"I don't agree with what you have been saying, Pierre," said Edmond Souturier, who had not hitherto taken part in the discussion.

"Men are brave," he continued, "when as soldiers they face death on the battlefield and as sailors fight against storm and shipwreck. Just as are the doctors who during an epidemic expose themselves to infection every moment of the day, and the missionaries who are in continual danger of being murdered by savages. We all appreciate the great courage shown by these men, don't we? But I am convinced there is not one of these who could swear that he has never been afraid. Fear is bred by certain mysterious influences and before vague dangers, which often fail to materialise. It comes from outside, and that is why it comes, above all, during the night, which changes familiar objects, giving them uncanny appearances. No one is proof against this sort of fear."

"Indeed," cried Pierre. "In spite of what you say, I swear that I would keep calm, however spooky my surroundings!"

"Very well, then. Are you willing to take on a bet?" asked Edmond.

"Yes, rather."

"Then I suggest that we take you to the Boulevard de La Chapelle, or better still to somewhere near Père-Lachaise. We will leave you there for the night, and in the morning will expect you to tell us quite frankly if you have been afraid."

"That won't do," said Pierre, smiling. "I shall meet with material danger there in the form of apaches, and I don't relish being stabbed to prove to you that I am fearless!"

"All right then," replied Edmond Souturier. "What about a night in the cemetery itself among the tombstones? You might see some of the ghosts which terrorised Jacques' infancy!"

"Surely that is locked up at night?"

"We can bribe the gatekeeper."

"I daresay, but it's no joke getting thoroughly wet through and finishing up with an attack of pneumonia!"

"I thought as much; you are trying to get out of it!"

"Not at all, but find something more to my taste. Let me see, what can I suggest? A horrible place, but where I can keep dry."

"A night shelter?"

"No thank you. They swarm with vermin."

"A public house in the Faubert district?"

"There again there is the danger of being knifed!"

"A den – or a low dance hall?"

"Good Lord no! None of these will fill me with the fear of the unknown."

"I have it!" cried Jacques. "The waxwork museum!"

"I didn't know there was one. Where is it?" questioned Edmond.

"What! Do you mean to tell me that you haven't seen it at the Montmartre Fair? It is the most horrible place you can possibly imagine! All the celebrated crimes are represented there, and there are also reproductions of executions, drinking and opium dens and the dregs of society, all fashioned in a yellowish wax which makes you feel quite sick. I visited it in broad daylight, but soon hurried out!"

"Where is it now?"

"Still at Montmartre. Only it has moved from Boulevard Rochechouart to Saint Pierre."

"Are you positive?"

"Yes. I went that way yesterday, and it was still there."

"Does that suit you?" asked Edmond.

"Yes, it sounds just the thing. It will only be a question of tipping the manager."

They settled their bill and were surprised to find that it was ten-thirty. No one had noticed the time during the absorbing discussion.

While waiting for a taxi Jacques drew Pierre aside, saying, "Are you in dead earnest?"

"Why, of course," replied Pierre.

"I wish you wouldn't go," pleaded Jacques. "I have a queer feeling something terrible will happen to you!"

"Don't be an old woman, Jacques!"

"By the way," said Edmond, joining them. "How much will you bet me?"

"Is twenty-five louis enough?" said Pierre.

"Done," replied Edmond. "The conditions are that you will spend the whole night in the waxwork museum, and tomorrow you will tell us quite truthfully whether you were frightened or not."

"I promise to do exactly as you say," said Pierre, laughing as usual.

They started off. It was not raining so much, and the wind had subsided a little, but when at last they arrived at their destination it was utterly deserted. The awful weather which had kept the sightseers at home had driven the proprietor to take shelter in a wine shop, where they eventually found him.

Edmond proceeded to explain the object of their visit, but at first the showman refused to show any interest, evidently suspecting burglary. However, the sight of a small wad of notes overruled his objections, and he agreed reluctantly to take Pierre to the museum.

The others went with him as far as the entrance, where they wished him good-night.

Jacques and Louis hailed a cab and set off homewards, whilst Edmond remarked that he was going to finish up the night by dancing in Montmartre.

Pierre followed the showman, who, with a lantern in his hand, opened the door and pushed aside a curtain. He led the way down some rickety steps through the boards of which the rain had oozed, making them dangerously slippery. He raised the lantern so that Pierre could see the surroundings.

A livid glare revealed the reproduction of the assassination of Gouffé. Pierre restrained a desire to laugh as he gazed at the figure of the poor wretched man, half suspended in the air with his tongue hanging out of his mouth; whilst the hangman, his veins swollen with the effort, pulled the rope.

The man walked slowly, stopping frequently to flash his light on some fresh horror. One scene carried out exactly the picture which Pierre had evoked in the restaurant. A deserted street in a distant quarter – a winter's night – the murderer hiding in a dark corner and pouncing out on the unfortunate wayfarer.

The obscure artist who had modelled all these heads must have been gifted with a very highly developed sense of horror. He had given to the murderer a particularly sinister and brutal expression, and to the murdered the most repulsive contortion of features that can be betrayed by death which has come in some terrible manner. Pierre was highly amused and, in order to please the man, complimented him on the models.

Next there came a row of grimacing heads belonging to ten or so celebrated people who had been guillotined. They were resting on blue velvet stands and leaning forward a little exposing the severed section. Lined up as on parade and fashioned in dirty coloured wax with decayed, tobacco-stained teeth showing through long, drooping whiskers, they hardly made a pleasant picture.

At the end of this mournful row stood a guillotine under which was stretched the decapitated body of a man. The knife was a dull crimson and his head lay in the basket. This was followed by a series of tableaux representative of the man's life from his early days to the events leading to the gallows!

"We can't go any further," said the man, "so I will leave you the lantern. I can find my way back in the dark."

But Pierre, anxious to win his bet, refused the loan of the light.

The showman departed and he was left alone. Somewhere in the surrounding blackness a clock struck midnight. It had stopped raining, but the wind, although quieter, moaned and whistled, inflating the canvas walls, which enhanced the unwholesome atmosphere.

He lit a match and found a chair; buttoning his overcoat about his neck he sat down with the intention of going to sleep. His thoughts wandered to his friends, who were by now snug between their blankets, and he shivered a little. How the dreary hours until dawn were going to drag!

He got up and lighting a cigarette began to stroll up and down; from time to time stopping in front of a glass case where the red glow from the cigarette end revealed the pale faces of his weird companions, but somehow he no longer found them amusing. They irritated him, and tired of walking he went back to his chair and sat down again; something pressed against him, and feeling in his pocket he found the small loaded revolver, which he always carried at night. This he transferred to his overcoat pocket and shut his eyes.

He had dozed for some fifteen or twenty minutes when he was awoken with a start by a violent gust of wind. What was that moving? It sounded like footsteps. He strained his ears and, lighting a match, peered round the museum. For a few seconds the malignant evil faces leered at him. "Oh! My God, what hideous things!" he exclaimed, and began to feel desperately depressed.

Unable to sit still he wandered about again, and in his confusion jostled against something cold and hard. Putting out his hand to steady himself he realised with repugnance that he had touched the knife of the guillotine! Swaying a little he lit another match; the faint beam of light betrayed the figure of a man who seemed to be towering above him holding a knife in his hand! The match flickered out and darkness once more enveloped him. He lit another: now he was in front of the grinning heads! The moan of the wind reminded him of the sighing of lost souls.

"Pull yourself together," he cried aloud. "It is ridiculous to be frightened. Fancy letting the cold get the better of you!" As he spoke a rat raced across the floor, uttering little sharp cries. It scrambled on to the boards which supported the wax figures, and disappeared.

The clock chimed. Pierre listened intently, convinced that he heard the noise of footsteps; it sounded as though someone were pacing the museum. It was utterly dark. The wind swelled the canvas.

He found himself picturing his gruesome room-mates, and their frightful faces took feverish possession of his brain. He no longer wondered if he was afraid. He knew that fear was gaining on him! An unreasonable and foolish fear which he was determined to conquer. He struck a third match and held it up, forcing himself to look round. He closed his eyes instantly, all the livid faces seemed to have become alive and were fixing him with a glassy stare; they were repellent and contorted.

A cold sweat gathered on his forehead. He swivelled round, surely something had touched him? This was horrible – more than he could bear – he must get out. Fearfully he stumbled towards the little staircase, but to his dismay found that the door was locked. He tried shaking it, but it was sufficiently strong to make it impossible for him to break it open. He realised with frightful sureness that he was a prisoner until the morning. Staggering back to the museum he lit another match, but the sight was more than he could stand, and he hastily blew it out, throwing it on the floor.

It was raining a little again and the wind was still moaning. Suddenly a shrill whistle rent the air, echoing round the room; it repeated itself twice, then still, unbroken silence reigned. A ghastly, intense silence, which seemed heavy and menacing, full of the unknown. He dared not stir, and horrible visions of the assassinated Gouffé floated across his mind. He was haunted by the swollen, lolling tongue, and the guillotine looking calmly down on the decapitated body.

Now he was sure someone was lurking outside the museum. He tried speaking aloud to reassure himself, but the sound of his tremulous voice only served to make the atmosphere worse, and the words stuck in his throat, so that he was forced to relapse into silence.

A fresh terror overcame him. He was certain all the wax figures were moving towards him, crowding round to stifle him. It was airless, and he put out his hands to push them away. His teeth chattered, and he was rooted to the spot.

A chuckle rang through the museum. It came from the direction of the line of horrid heads! His heart pounding like a sledge hammer he turned swiftly, expecting an onslaught from the unseen enemy, and clutched convulsively at his revolver.

There was complete silence again for a few seconds, until suddenly the chuckle was repeated.

His strength gave way. The fear of being smothered by the figures had increased; they must be getting very close now. The minutes seemed like eternity. He tried to reason with himself, arguing that he was unnerved by the awful dark silence, and that he had imagined he heard the noise. He breathed more easily, but only for a few moments, for now, again, the mocking chuckle echoed. This time he realised that it had been no trick of his imagination. That last laugh had been near him. He must find out where it came from.

Taking his courage in both hands he lighted one of his matches and looked. He saw "it" at once above the row of guillotined heads. It was another head grimacing like the rest! Haggard and pale with a wagging tongue! Good God! This decapitated head was beginning to move! It was alive! He could bear it no longer, and drawing out his revolver, fired.

A little blood spurted from the forehead as the head fell upon the others!

Pierre, grasping his revolver, fell fainting on the floor.

Early next morning the showman, arriving to release Pierre, tripped over a body which was stretched across the ground. He recoiled, horror-struck, seeing a bullet wound in the forehead. He tried to lift the body, but soon realised it was futile, for the man was stone dead!

Aware that he could do nothing he looked round, and noticed that the canvas which covered the flimsy structure of the museum had a large tear in it just above the row of guillotined heads, and that a little blood had reddened them!

He leant through the rent and called out. No one answered. He ran quickly to the door and unlocked it. Lying in a crumpled heap on the floor was the young man he had shut up in the museum the night before.

He hurried in and tried to raise Pierre, but before he had time to dodge aside the boy had hurled himself at him and was trying to strangle him. His brain had been turned! Hearing the man's cries people came to his aid, and they managed, with some difficulty, to overpower the madman.

The inquest revealed the name of the dead man to be Edmond Souturier. It was he who, in the middle of the night, tried to frighten his friend for a joke in the hope that he would win his bet. He had passed his head through the canvas covering, leering and chuckling, but he also was turned into a wax figure!

THE REAL OPERA GHOST

THE OPERA GHOST really existed. He was not, as was long believed, a creature of the imagination of the artists, the superstition of the managers, or a product of the absurd and impressionable brains of the young ladies of the ballet, their mothers, the box-keepers, the cloakroom attendants or the concierge. Yes, he existed in flesh and blood, although he assumed the complete appearance of a real phantom; that is to say of a spectral shade.

When I began to ransack the archives of the National Academy of Music I was at once struck by the surprising coincidences between the phenomena ascribed to the "ghost" and the most extraordinary and fantastic tragedy that ever excited the Paris upper classes; and I soon conceived the idea that this tragedy might reasonably be explained by the phenomena in question. The events do not date more than thirty years back; and it would not be difficult to find at the present day, in the foyer of the ballet, old men of the highest respectability, men upon whose word one could absolutely rely, who would remember as though they happened yesterday the mysterious and dramatic conditions that attended the kidnapping of Christine Daaé, the disappearance of the Vicomte de Chagny and the death of his elder brother, Count Philippe, whose body was found on the bank of the lake that exists in the lower cellars of the Opera on the Rue Scribe side. But none of those witnesses had until that day thought that there was any reason for connecting the more or less legendary figure of the Opera ghost with that terrible story.

The truth was slow to enter my mind, puzzled by an inquiry that at every moment was complicated by events which, at first sight, might be looked upon as superhuman; and more than once I was within an ace of abandoning a task in which I was exhausting myself in the hopeless pursuit of a vain image. At last, I

received the proof that my presentiments had not deceived me,
and I was rewarded for all my efforts on the day when I acquired
the certainty that the Opera ghost was more than a mere shade.

On that day, I had spent long hours over *The Memoirs of a
Manager,* the light and frivolous work of the too-sceptical
Moncharmin, who, during his term at the Opera, understood
nothing of the mysterious behaviour of the ghost and who was
making all the fun of it that he could at the very moment when he
became the first victim of the curious financial operation that
went on inside the "magic envelope".

I had just left the library in despair, when I met the delightful
acting manager of our National Academy, who stood chatting on
a landing with a lively and well-groomed little old man, to whom
he introduced me gaily. The acting manager knew all about my
investigations and how eagerly and unsuccessfully I had been
trying to discover the whereabouts of the examining magistrate
in the famous Chagny case, M. Fauré. Nobody knew what had
become of him, alive or dead; and here he was back from
Canada, where he had spent fifteen years, and the first thing he
had done, on his return to Paris, was to come to the secretarial
offices at the Opera and ask for a free seat. The little old man was
M. Fauré himself.

We spent a good part of the evening together and he told me
the whole Chagny case as he had understood it at the time. He
was bound to conclude in favour of the madness of the viscount
and the accidental death of the elder brother, for lack of evidence
to the contrary; but he was nevertheless persuaded that a terrible
tragedy had taken place between the two brothers in connection
with Christine Daaé. He could not tell me what became of
Christine or the viscount. When I mentioned the ghost, he only
laughed. He, too, had been told of the curious manifestations
that seemed to point to the existence of an abnormal being,
residing in one of the most mysterious corners of the Opera, and
he knew the story of the envelope; but he had never seen anything in it worthy of his attention as magistrate in charge of
the Chagny case, and all he had done had been to listen to the
evidence of a witness who appeared of his own accord and

declared that he had often met the ghost. This witness was none other than the man whom all Paris called the "Persian" and who was well known to every subscriber to the Opera. The magistrate took him for a visionary.

I was immensely interested by this story of the Persian. I wanted, if there were still time, to find this valuable and eccentric witness. My luck began to improve and I discovered him in his little flat in the Rue de Rivoli, where he had lived ever since and where he died five months after my visit. I was at first inclined to be suspicious; but when the Persian had told me, with childlike candour, all that he knew about the ghost and had handed me the proofs of the ghost's existence – including the strange correspondence of Christine Daaé – to do as I pleased with, I was no longer able to doubt. No, the ghost was not a myth!

I have, I know, been told that this correspondence may have been forged from first to last by a man whose imagination had certainly been fed on the most seductive tales; but fortunately I discovered some of Christine's writing outside the famous bundle of letters and, on a comparison between the two, all my doubts were removed. I also went into the past history of the Persian and found that he was an upright man, incapable of inventing a story that might have defeated the ends of justice.

This, moreover, was the opinion of the more serious people who, at one time or another, were mixed up in the Chagny case, who were friends of the Chagny family, to whom I showed all my documents and set forth all my inferences. In this connection, I should like to print a few lines which I received from General D——:

Sir:

I cannot urge you too strongly to publish the results of your inquiry. I remember perfectly that, a few weeks before the disappearance of that great singer, Christine Daaé, and the tragedy which threw the whole of the Faubourg Saint-Germain into mourning, there was a great deal of talk, in the foyer of the ballet, on the subject of the "ghost"; and I believe that it only ceased to be discussed in consequence of the later affair that excited us all so greatly. But, if it be possible – as, after hearing you, I believe – to explain the tragedy through the ghost, then I beg you, sir, to talk to us about the ghost again. Mysterious though the ghost may at first appear, he will always be more easily explained than the dismal story in which malevolent people have tried to picture two brothers killing each other who had worshipped each other all their lives.

Believe me, etc.

Lastly, with my bundle of papers in hand, I once more went over the ghost's vast domain, the huge building which he had made his kingdom. All that my eyes saw, all that my mind perceived, corroborated the Persian's documents precisely; and a wonderful discovery crowned my labours in a very definite fashion. It will be remembered that, later, when digging in the substructure of the Opera, before burying the phonographic records of the artist's voice, the workmen laid bare a corpse. Well, I was at once able to prove that this corpse was that of the Opera ghost. I made the acting manager put this proof to the test with his own hand; and it is now a matter of supreme indifference to me if the papers pretend that body was that of a victim of the Commune.

The wretches who were massacred, under the Commune, in the cellars of the Opera, were not buried on this side; I will tell you where their skeletons can be found in a spot not very far from that immense crypt which was stocked during the siege with all sorts of provisions. I came upon this track just when I was looking for the remains of the Opera ghost, which I should never have discovered but for the unheard-of chance described above.